Tennant brought both hands out from his vest. His left cupped a silver matchbox that he flung straight at the tall man's face. His right brought out a tiny Remington over-and-under derringer.

The tall man shifted his head to the side,
letting the sil… glance off his cheek. At the
same time h… is hip.

It was a S… an, the grip
plated with … frame chased
with polish… nd top latch
were scrub… ne.

The shin… last of smoke
as the .44 … ew Tennant
exactly on…

The slu… muscle of the
stomach. … r rim of the pelvic
girdle, a… der Tennant's
ribs . . .

Also in the Gunslinger series in Sphere Books:

THE MASSACRE TRAIL
THE GOLDEN GUN
THE WHITE APACHE
50 CALIBRE KILL
ARIZONA BLOODLINE
REBEL VENGEANCE
DEATH CANYON
PEACEMAKER

Gunslinger: The Russian Lode

CHARLES C. GARRETT

SPHERE BOOKS LIMITED
30–32 Gray's Inn Road, London WC1X 8JL

First published by Sphere Books Ltd 1980

Slingers of words and guns – but mostly of enthusiasm – for which we all thank them: Dave Whitehead and Mike Stotter. With friendship.

TRADE
MARK

Set in Monotype Baskerville

Printed and bound in Great Britain by
©ollins, Glasgow

Chapter One

Tucson was quiet. On a Wednesday it mostly was: especially at the middle of the month. Especially during the Spring round-up time.

It was too early – or too late – for the hands to come in off the surrounding ranches like they did when the Winter lay-off gave them time to spare, or the lush Summer grass held the cows close to the good pastures. They didn't get paid until the end of the month; and what little they had to spend in the Spring got blown at the end of the week, when hoarded money or argued advances could buy whisky and women on a blurred weekend that left the few lucky enough to enjoy the fleshpots of the town riding back with red-rimmed eyes and liquor-blown memories of the pleasures of a town.

The stage still came through twice a week. Once on the long swing west through Arizona to California. Then again on the dog-leg back to the East, cutting through to New Mexico before dividing the passengers heading for Texas from those going on to Kansas or Missouri or Illinois.

And every once in a while the stage dropped people off in Tucson. People who were drummers, or saloon girls, or just travellers.

The man who climbed down from the drop-step with the noonday sun shining light off the sweat beading his face was a traveller. Beard stubble held the beads of moisture close against his angular jaw. He looked hot – sweaty – but the first thing he did when he stepped into the dust of mainstreet was to hike his black coat back clear of the gun holstered on his right hip and check the slide of pistol against leather.

Then he looked up and down the street, hiding his movement under the pretence of wiping a bandanna across his face. And moved automatically into the shade of the porch, where the overhanging verandah of Dolly Harman's *What Cheer* saloon could hide him from the bright, burning glare of the sun.

The guard on the Concord tossed a small valise down, and the man caught it with the deft movement of long practice, cradling it under his left arm as he watched the coach roll away down the street. Then he pushed in through the batwings and went up to the bar. He ducked his head as he went through the doorway.

'Beer.' His voice was soft, the last syllable rolling into a slur. 'Then whisky.'

He downed a mug of beer in one long swallow. Called for a second as he sipped the harder liquor. Then took his time over the next, eyes scanning the long room that made up the central part of the *What Cheer*.

In the afternoon, in the middle of the week, in Spring, there weren't too many people there. Down the end of the room a few townsfolk were taking their midday meal. Store-owners, mostly, or ranchers come in to discuss business with the new banker who had taken over when Goldburgh got killed*.

The sole difference from any other of the many townships the man had seen was the group of card players over against the far wall.

See *Gunslinger 5 – Arizona Bloodline

There were four of them. Each one had a glass in front, the whisky forming dark rings on the baize topping. There was a bottle at the centre, alongside the pile of chips.

But no one was playing the game.

Instead, they were listening to the dark-haired man seated against the wall. His voice was a low murmur that didn't carry further than his immediate circle of companions. He held his cards folded close against his chest. The others were letting theirs show as they gaped at the speaker.

From where the tall man in the black suit lounged casually against the bar the cards were in clear view, spread out in surprise and greed. One player held a matched set of pairs; another carried a useless mixture of random cards; the last held a flush that folded slowly on to the table as the dark-haired man went on parlaying his spiel.

The man at the bar emptied his beer mug and then tipped down the whisky. He turned to the barkeep.

'I want a room.'

Ben Turner nodded and said, 'Two dollar room, or a four dollar special?'

'At the front. Bath, too.'

'Got one looks right over the entrance. For a dollar extra, I'll fix the bath to be brought up.'

Turner grinned: 'Five more can fix a real good scrubbing. Dolly got a Chinese girl in a while ago. Knows all the secrets of the Orient. Things you ain't never experienced.'

'Forget it.' The tall man shook his head. 'Just hike the bath up there. That and a bottle of good whisky.'

There was something in his voice that stopped Ben from pushing the wares of the *What Cheer* any further. Instead, he fumbled under the bar for the key and passed it over to the big man.

'Number seven,' he said. 'Take the door on yore left an' head along the corridor.'

'Thanks.' The man took the key and lifted his valise in his left hand. 'Get that bath ready.'

'Yessir! Right away.'

Somehow Ben didn't feel like arguing.

The room was small and hot. There was a narrow bed banged up against the window to the left side of the saloon's door. A washstand with a jug of dirty water, flies floating on the surface, beside the bed. A few hooks on the facing wall, and a porcelain bowl under the bed. The porcelain was cracked and the pot gave off a sour odour.

The man stripped down to his undershirt, hanging his vest and pants on the hooks. Wearing only a sweat-stained set of longjohns, he began opening up his valise.

It contained a second gun and an oil-skin pouch of tools and cleaning equipment, along with a spare shirt and extra underwear. The gun kit took up most of the room in the small bag.

Spreading a cloth square on the bed he began to check over his two pistols, stripping them down to the component parts before oiling them very carefully and reassembling the delicate mechanisms. After that he checked each cartridge, sliding six into the pistol he holstered on his belt, and five into the spare pistol kept in his valise.

A tapping at the door announced the arrival of his tub, and he swung the thin partition inwards. Holding the frame with his left hand, he stepped back so that the door partly shielded him. The loaded revolver was in his right hand, muzzle at hip height. The young Mexican carrying the zinc tub glanced warily at the black mouth of the gun and set the bath down in a hurry. Behind him an elderly Chinaman turned pale eyes on the gunman and whistled softly between his teeth. He ignored the implied danger with the stoicism of the Orient as he tipped a bucket of steaming water into the receptacle and folded a towel neatly on the bed.

The man waited until the Mexican and the Chinese returned with more water and two pails of cold, still standing just inside the small room with the pistol angled into the corridor.

When the bath was full, steam curling in lazy clouds through the warm air, he locked the door. Then he opened the window and thrust his head out, scanning the sidewalk. The street was empty save for a few old men playing moon around an upturned barrel, and a grizzled grey dog that was gnawing on a bone under the far porch. The man left the window open, but drew the grubby curtains. Then he cocked the revolver and set it on the floor beside the tub. Stripped out of his longjohns. And climbed into the water.

He was a big man. Too big for the tub, so that he was forced to bend his knees and assume a crouched position that left his belly and torso clear of the water. His skin was pale, the puckered redness of scar tissue showing where bullets had pierced his right shoulder, left arm, and left hip. Down the right side of his face, running from the greying hair of his temple to the corner of his wide mouth, there was a fine, white scar. A knife wound. He rubbed it absently as he luxuriated in the cleansing warmth, then picked up the soap and began to scrub his muscular body.

It had been a long time since the last bath, and the cooling water assumed a grey colour, the surface collecting a scum of whitish froth.

When he was finished he stood up, dousing himself in the cold water, then climbed out and began to towel dry.

He dug clean underwear and a fresh shirt from his valise. The underwear was bright red; the shirt white. He pulled on black pants; black boots; buttoned his black vest over his flat stomach. Then he buckled the gunbelt tight around his waist. Tied the holster down on his right leg and dropped the pistol inside. The holster and belt were shiny, oiled leather: better tended than his clothes. He shrugged into his coat and settled a flat-crowned black stetson on his head.

Then he pushed the valise under the bed and left the room.

Ben Turner looked up from the newspaper he was reading as the man approached. Something about his manner prompted Ben to slide both hands under the bar where they touched the comforting shape of the sawn-off Remington shotgun kept there.

'You forgot my whisky.' Grey eyes bored, unblinking, into Ben's. 'I don't like people who forget things.'

'Jesus!' Ben's forefinger curled nervously around the trigger of the scattergun. 'I'm sorry, mister. You want it now?'

The man shook his head. 'No. Just remember that when I ask for something I expect to get it. I don't expect to ask twice.'

'Nosir!' Ben nodded, wondering what a hardcase like this was doing in Tucson on a quiet Wednesday. 'I'll not forget again.'

'Don't,' grunted the man.

And walked out into the afternoon heat.

He paced down the sidewalk, steps surprisingly light for so big a man. So light they made hardly any sound on the sun-weathered boards. His head remained forwards, tilted slightly so that the black stetson shaded most of his face. But his eyes drifted constantly from left to right, and back again. Checking. Watching.

And his right hand stayed close to the butt of the pistol.

He located the barber shop and found an empty chair. Draping his coat over the back, he settled down and called for a shave. As the cloth settled about him, he eased his revolver from the holster and rested the gun between his knees.

One hour later he emerged with a fresh-shaved face and a haircut. His boots were polished to a shine that danced the sun's light back at the sky. And he smelled faintly of lavender water.

He went into the Rickarts' eatery, calling for steak and hash greens. Anne Rickarts opened her mouth to tell him that they were closed until evening, then changed her mind and asked her husband to serve him. Dave Rickarts looked out through the kitchen hatch and began to cook. He didn't serve the food himself, leaving that duty to the wandering lawyer they had taken on as waiter after he turned up beaten black by some itinerant owlhooter.

The man ate his food at a measured pace, chewing each mouthful as carefully as if it was his last. He drank four cups of coffee, and settled his bill with high-shining coins of the latest vintage.

It was around five when he left. The sun was still heating Tucson, though now it was spreading dark shadows along the streets, cut off from the alleyways flanking the main drag so that they were plunged into a dim half-light where dust danced in the air and lazy dogs sought comfort from the heat.

The man turned down one such alley, following the signs that pointed to Gus Traver's stable.

He went in through the man-sized door cut alongside the main opening. And began checking over the horses before Gus woke up from his customary nap.

By the time the stablehand was fully awake, his unexpected customer had a tall bay stallion out in the central aisle and was checking over the animal's points. He turned as Gus emerged from his tiny office, right hand dropping to the butt of his pistol.

'He ain't fer sale.' Gus walked forwards, scrubbing at his eyes and wiping the rheum down his shirtfront. 'Belongs to Mort Gannon. An' Mort reckons him the finest horse in Arizona.'

'He could be right,' said the man, slurring the *t* into a soft sound. 'I want him.'

'I told you he ain't fer sale,' grumbled Gus. 'You want a horse, I got some good stock out back. Mustangs, Quarter Horses, even a Morgan. Give over a good price, too.'

The man shook his head: 'I want this one.'

'Christ Jesus!' Gus dug a finger into his left ear. Examined the findings, and flicked them away. 'That one ain't fer sale! How many times you need telling?'

'Just once,' said the man. 'I remember things. The same way I expect folks to remember what I say. I want this horse.'

'You can't have him.' Gus kicked straw from the stable's floor. 'That pony's worth around one hundred dollars. I can sell you a mount fer twenty. No more'n fifty if you fancy the Morgan.'

'I'll take this one.'

The tall man reached over to drape the bridle around the post.

Then he slung a saddle over the bay and hiked a knee hard against the stallion's belly so that the animal sucked in its breath and let him fasten the girth straps tight over the ribs.

Gus picked up a pitchfork and stumbled forwards:

'You ain't nothin' but a goddam horsethief! You back off now!'

The tall man in the black outfit laughed.

Drew his gun.

And shot Gus Traver through the belly.

The old man staggered back, feet dancing under the impact of the bullet. The pitchfork flew loose from his hands, curling through the dim air to imbed ten feet behind him. The tines set up a dull thrumming.

The man walked forwards and shot Gus in the face. The slug ruptured the nose, shattering the fragile bones so that they exploded inwards, collapsing the eye sockets and the upper lip into a single, massive hole that had once been a face.

The straw covering the stable's floor got sticky with blood. Gus Traver voided his last connection with life and lay still amongst the mess of his own body.

The gunman climbed up on the bay stallion and walked the big horse up to the stable doors. He dismounted just long enough to open the doors and take the horse through. Then he tossed two lanterns down the aisle. Waiting until the kerosene was spreading over the straw.

And fired twice.

Each bullet ignited the fuel, spreading flames along the length of the stable. The central space burst into fire that crept up over the stalls in little, flickering tongues of darting flame. Yellow became red. Blue mixed in as manure heated and took flame. And the fire climbed over dry wood and stored grass.

Horses screamed, kicking against the stalls. Manes and tails began to burn as sparks fell down from the loft and a raw wall of fire ran down through the stable.

The gunman rode down the alley and dismounted outside the *What Cheer*.

The crackle of the flames was already pulling people out on to the street: impromptu fire fighters were pumping water and hauling buckets towards the burning stable. The saloon was mostly empty.

Except for the card players.

The same quartet was still bunched around the table. Still listening to the dark-haired man. The only differences were the empty whisky bottle and the forgotten cards. No one held anything now – except glasses – and they were ignored as the dark-haired man went on talking.

The tall man in the black suit went up to the bar and reached over for the bottle Ben Turner had left when he ran out to help fight the fire. He poured a measure into a clean glass and drank it as he studied the paper he tugged from his inside pocket.

The sheet was worn where it had been folded, the creases blanched out into tear-lines so that the thing was punctuated with ragged holes. He stared at it, not really needing to study the words again, but enjoying the feeling of anticipation now that his quarry was so near.

Neat writing covered the sheet where it was not broken by the folds. There was no name at the top, nor any signature at the bottom. Only the carefully-scribed hand that had penned the message:

Matthew Tennant is around thirty years old. He has

dark hair and dark eyes. Clean shaved. Women say he is handsome. He talks a lot and favours dark clothing. He carries a pocket pistol in his vest, but he is not a gunman.

He travels with his wife, who is a pretty woman of about twenty-five years' age. She has auburn hair and eyes the colour of chestnuts. Do not harm her!

Kill Tennant, and I will pay you the $3000 promised.

You know where to come.

The man folded the note and tucked it back inside his coat.

He eased his pistol against the oiled leather of the holster and went over to the table. The men seated there did not spot him until he was standing behind the nearest player.

Then his voice cut through the buzz of their conversation:

'You're Matthew Tennant, ain't you?'

The dark-haired man looked up and grinned nervously.

'I got christened that. Why?'

'You're a goddam cardsharp. You're a cheat an' a liar. A coward, too.'

Tennant shrugged, hiking his thumbs into the pockets of his vest.

'I don't know you, friend. Nor want to. You got me mixed up with someone else.'

'No.' The tall man shook his head. 'Only thing I might mix you with is a buzzard. Picking over other folk's bones.' He shifted his cold eyes sideways to encompass the three curious men around the table. 'Be best if you moved clear, gents: I got no quarrel with you.'

They quit the table like rats leaving a drowning ship.

Tennant asked, 'Why? Who sent you?'

'That matter?' The tall man reached his left hand round to tug his coat clear of his gun. 'You're gonna die anyway.'

'The hell I am!' Tennant brought both hands out from his vest. His left cupped a silver matchbox that he flung straight at the tall man's face. His right brought out a tiny Remington over-and-under derringer.

The tall man shifted his head to the side, letting the silver box glance off his cheek. At the same time he drew the pistol on his hip.

It was a Smith & Wesson Russian, the grip plated with ivory, the straps and frame chased with polished silver. The barrel and top latch were scrubbed to a matching shine.

The shine got lost under the blast of smoke as the .44 calibre slug hit Matthew Tennant exactly one inch above his belt.

The slug went in through the muscle of the stomach. Glanced off the upper rim of the pelvic girdle, and tore loose from under Tennant's ribs.

Tennant opened his mouth to scream, detonating the Remington into the floor as he was plucked backwards by the force of the close-fired shot. The tall man fired again, his second bullet tearing through Tennant's ribs to deflect off the clavicle and plunge upwards into the neck.

Tennant choked on blood and pain. Where he struck the wall, there was a red smear flecked through with white shards of bone.

The gunman snapped open the catch holding the cylinder against the butt plate: all six shells sprang loose, expelled by the interior spring. He held the broken pistol in his right hand, thumbing fresh shells into the chambers with his left. Then he snapped the thing closed, cylinder tucking neatly down as the retaining catch fell against the upper bar of the cylinder frame.

'You all saw it.' He addressed himself to the three men staring at Tennant's corpse. 'He was reaching for that derringer. I killed him fair.'

No one spoke as he holstered the Smith & Wesson and went down to his room.

As the door swung shut behind him, all three went running on to the street, shouting for the law.

Sheriff Nolan came running back from the burning stable with one hand holding a Colt's Navy model and the other supporting his gut. He paused across the street from the *What Cheer*, wondering why three of the most prominent citizens were hollering so loud and why Mort Gannon's big bay stallion was hitched outside when Mort was busy helping fight the blaze and wondering about his prize pony.

Then he saw the black-suited man climb into the saddle and took a long, deep breath. For a moment he wished he didn't eat so much, but then he thought about the star pinned to his food-stained shirt and went forwards with the Navy Colt lifting up to point on the man's chest.

'Hold it, mister!'

As he said it, he knew that his voice was too hoarse and winded to carry far. Too wasted by too much food and too much liquor. He lifted the Colt, bracing his shoulders so that the late sun lit up the badge.

Then roared as the man triggered one shot that went in through the fleshy part of Nolan's shoulder, spinning the fat lawman round so that his own pistol emptied a chamber into the sky while the man rode off at full gallop down mainstreet.

Nolan felt his butt hit the dirt. Felt tears squeeze past his eyelids. And felt fire burn horribly through his shoulder as the big bay disappeared southwards and Dolly Harman came running from across the street.

As the darkness closed in he fought to retain some identifying mark, some means of pointing out the killer. As Dolly's hands clutched him he found it: the man's gun. He had never seen a gun like that before. It had looked like a Smith & Wesson, but there had been a curved spur under the trigger guard, the gunman's second finger hooking round the underslung curve to steady the pistol as he fired. Nolan had never seen a gunslinger use that kind of weapon.

Then the fire in his arm took hold like the flames that were consuming the stable and he slumped back, letting his head drop over Dolly's wide-spread legs.

Chapter Two

Seven people attended the funeral. And none cried.

Four were grave-diggers, the fifth the undertaker – who liked to see a job done all the way through. The sixth was Nolan, right arm swathed in a bandage that was flecked with food stains and clinging particles of bread and chilli. The seventh was the widow: Laura Tennant.

She was tall, her body straight and firm, breasts thrusting out the bodice of the dark blue dress. She wore a bonnet with a black veil, but the mesh was pushed back in deference to the heat so that clear, tearless, brown eyes were visible above a straight nose and a wide, full-lipped mouth. A few curls of reddish-brown hair hung about her slender neck.

She watched the coffin lowered into the pit and reached down to scoop a handful of soil. It was dry and crumbly. It rattled on the cheap pine of the box.

'You want to say a few words, ma'am?' The undertaker felt the occasion wasn't quite right without a preacher. 'Be fitting.'

'Goodbye, Matt. You went down for the last time.'

She turned away, ignoring the curious stares of the six men.

'Hell!' Nolan turned to follow her. 'Get him covered, boys.'

The undertaker nodded at the grave-diggers, who began to spade earth in a steady torrent over the casque. He settled his fresh-polished beaver on his head and climbed sedately on to the high seat of the black-draped hearse. Dyed plumes rustled as the four horses shook their heads, and the death wagon rolled regally down the long slope that lead into Tucson. It halted outside the *What Cheer*.

Nolan handed the woman on to the seat of a buggy and climbed awkwardly up behind her. His stomach rumbled: it was close on noon.

Picking up the reins, the overweight lawman said, 'I sent a few men out last night, Mizz Tennant, but they lost him. Was too dark to trail proper.'

The woman nodded, adjusting the veil about her face as they approached the town.

'I want him found, Sheriff. I'll put up five thousand dollars for the man who brings him in with proof he killed my husband.'

Nolan belched nervously. 'That's a lot o' money, ma'am.'

'My husband was worth a lot to me.' Primly. 'I want his killer brought to justice.'

'You mind me givin' a piece of advice?' Nolan was torn between the thought of the stew Dolly Harman had promised him and the problems of keeping the law in a Frontier town.

Laura Tennant shook her head. 'Please do. After all, you are the peace officer here.'

'Yeah.' Nolan wanted to scratch his shoulder, but he needed his good hand to steer the team. 'Fact is, ma'am, if you post that kinda reward you're gonna pull in every ready gun from here to Waco. Town'd get filled up with bounty hunters an' two-bit gunslingers. There'd be trouble burstin' all over.'

'You had trouble last night.' Her voice was cold. 'And that was caused by just one man.'

'Yeah.' The itch on Nolan's shoulder got worse.

'But like you say, I am the peace officer. I'd sooner avoid that kinda problem.'

'Which still leaves us with the original cause.' She stared straight ahead, expression hidden by the veil. 'And I still want my husband's murderer brought in.'

'I know one man might do it.' Nolan wriggled his shoulder. The pain the movement caused made him forget the itch. 'Man called Ryker. John Ryker. Some folks call him Black Jack Ryker.'

'He's good?' The coldness left her voice, replaced by interest. 'He could find the man?'

'If anyone can.' Nolan eased his arm down, glad that they were now inside of Tucson. 'Jack Ryker's about the best I know.'

Ryker tilted his hat down over his forehead, staring through the heat haze shrouding the town. He slowed the big black stallion he rode to a walking pace, letting the two ponies behind stumble into line.

Even through the canvas he had fastened around the outlaws the corpses were beginning to stink in the Spring heat.

He wondered what Nolan was doing in the buggy with a pretty woman. And who they had been burying.

Death interested Ryker: it was his business.

He rode down off the foothills and dismounted where the wind-washed fence marked the perimeter of the graveyard. The soil was still fresh and his approach sent three kites screaming into the sky. He studied the marker. It was a plain stone cross with a simple inscription: *Matthew Tennant, 1845–1874.*

Ryker climbed on to his horse and left the place to the carrion birds.

He followed the slope down into Tucson, ignoring the few townsfolk who watched him pass by. He was used to their comments by now – both adulatory, or damning – so they washed off him like water from the tail feathers of a duck.

It's Ryker . . . Black Jack Ryker . . . Goddam bounty hunter . . . Got some more goddam owlhooters where they belong . . . Killer . . . Deserved killing . . . Must be money on them . . . Weren't for him . . . Just for his bounty . . .

He reined in outside the *What Cheer* and glanced at the gold Hunter chained over his fancy vest. The hands stood at noon, and as the buggy he had watched was still outside the saloon, he knew that Nolan would be inside, eating.

He swung down and hitched the stallion to the post. Then hauled his black coat from behind the saddle and pushed in through the batwings.

Dolly Harman met him with a shriek of pure pleasure. Ryker opened his arms and wrapped them about her widening waist.

Scarlet skirt and lace petticoats swirled as he picked her up, exposing broad thighs that were topped with black garters. Breasts that were soft where the whalebone of her corsets didn't hold them in pressed against his chest, and carmined lips left a sticky mark on his face.

He set her down, dark eyes smiling a greeting: 'Good to see you, Dolly.'

'And you, Jack. Who you caught this time? I can smell the catch.'

Ryker grinned. 'Bodeen brothers. Not worth much, but Nolan should pay the reward.'

'The halfbreed and his kin?' Dolly frowned. 'You going for the small-game now? Two-Persons Bodeen an' his half-assed brother ain't worth shit.'

'I got to earn a living,' said Ryker. 'And they got a hundred apiece on them.'

'Scarce worth the trouble.' Dolly took his hand,

leading him over to the door at the side of the saloon, where the rooms were. 'Guess you wanta talk with that fat-assed sheriff.'

'And eat,' said Ryker. 'Unless he took it all.'

'Bring you the best I got.' Dolly fluttered heavy-mascara-ed lashes. 'Serve you myself.'

'Real grateful, Dolly.' Ryker went into the corridor. 'Where is he?'

'Usual place.' Dolly closed the door on her last words. 'Where he always is.'

Ryker went down to the end door. The one that led into Dolly's private rooms. Sheriff Nolan was spread around a table, one hand clutching a chewed taco, the other spooning chilli into his mouth. He burped as Ryker came in and smiled a spray of sauce over the table.

'Got the Bodeens outside,' said Ryker. 'What they worth?'

Nolan shrugged. 'Need to check the dodgers. Hundred?'

'Figured them for two,' grinned Ryker. 'That was the posting up north.'

'Jeez!' Nolan shovelled more food into his mouth, so that his answer came out on a spray of beans and gravy. 'You know the figgers better'n me. Two hundred, then. I could put you on to a five-thousand-dollar bounty.'

'Who?' Ryker sat down and poured himself a whisky from the lawman's bottle. 'I've not heard of no five-thousand-dollar outlaw.'

'Don't know his name.' Nolan scooped the plates in closer, piling the remnants of the meal into a single steaming mound. 'But he set the stable afire an' shot a man called Tennant without no provocation. The widow's putting up the five. An' I'd like you to earn it.'

'He do that?' Ryker pointed at the dirty bandage. 'That why you want me to trace him?'

Nolan shrugged as best he could with a broken shoulder, and said, 'Sure. Bastard put a slug through my arm after he burned Gus Traver. Besides, I still think you're the best.'

'Alive or dead?' Ryker emptied his glass. Filled a second. 'What leads you got.'

'The lady with the money don't mind how he comes in.' Nolan wiped up gravy with a solid wedge of home-baked bread. 'Only leads I got is how he looked an' the gun he used.'

Ryker's eyes got interested: 'Tell me.'

'Tall. Inch or so more'n you. Dark hair with grey on the sides. Wore a white shirt. No tie. He'd be around forty, but looked younger.'

The door opened and Dolly Harman came in with a tray of food. Nolan licked his lips as the succulent odour of charred steak filled the room.

'That's for Jack,' said the owner of the *What Cheer*. 'All of it.'

'He ain't never gonna manage a meal like that,' rumbled Nolan. 'Least I could do is take the pie off him.'

'Christ!' Dolly spread her arms wide in exasperation. 'Take it, you fat-uddered old tramp. I'll fetch Jack some more.'

'Don't forget the cream,' called Nolan as the door swung shut. 'You're gettin' a mite skimpy there.'

Dolly's reply got lost behind the smash of wood against frame.

'Don't ferget the gun,' said Ryker. 'What kind was it?'

'Don't rightly know.' The lawman scooped up the apple pie and began to spoon it into his mouth. 'I never saw one like it before. What I do know, I got from the fellers in the saloon with Tennant.'

'Describe it.' Ryker sipped coffee, his food forgotten. 'That's as good a way as any to trace a gunhand.'

'About the size of a Colt,' said Nolan. 'But the grip was smoother, not so much curve on it. Pearl, too. An' the metal was all shined up. Had a kinda small chamber an' a smooth-lookin' hammer, seemed to float back over the butt-plate.'

He paused, closing his eyes as he fought to retain the memories.

'Fellers as saw it used said the man just sprung it open, so all the shells come out at once. Hinged down under the barrel, they said. An' it had a funny kinda spur under the trigger. I saw his finger go round that when he shot me.'

'Smith & Wesson Russian,' said Ryker. 'They developed it off the American a year or so back. What more you know?'

'Not much.' Nolan watched the gunslinger swallow food with a hungry look. 'He didn't carry no rifle, but he was ridin' Mort Gannon's prize bay.'

Ryker forked up the last of his potatoes and pushed the plate over to Nolan. 'Where's this rich lady offering the reward?'

The sheriff gulped down the last of the greens and the grisle from the steak. Belched loudly, and eased his belly clear of the table.

'Got Dolly's best room. Waitin' to see you.'

Ryker shrugged into his coat. Fastened his string tie around the collar of his dirty white shirt, and set his hat on his head.

'Aren't they all?'

Nolan moved to follow him; until the gunslinger pointed down the corridor.

'You got two Bodeens waiting out there. Best bury

them. Then get my money ready.'

'You like me to stable yore horse, too?' asked Nolan.

"Thanks,' said Ryker. I'd appreciate that.'

And paced down the corridor to Laura Tennant's room.

Chapter Three

'Mister Ryker, I presume.'

For no particular reason he took off his hat, fingering the brim so that the silver dollar with the neat hole punched through the centre spun under his thumbs.

'Mrs Tennant? Sheriff Nolan said you needed someone.'

'I need a killer, Mister Ryker,' Her voice was calm and cool. And her face was lovely. 'Not a fancy gunman.'

Her eyes bored into Ryker's, then travelled down to the hat's brim. He lifted the stetson, answering the challenge.

'It's not a toy, ma'am. It's something I'm proud of.'

'A plugged coin? Anyone can bore a hole through a silver piece and call himself a gunman.'

'I shot that at one hundred paces, ma'am. What I can see, I can hit.'

'That's a big boast, Mister Ryker. Could you do it a second time?'

Ryker grinned: 'Would you hold it up?'

For a moment her eyes met his. Held; challenging. Then they slid back to the coin.

'I'm not so foolish as to hold targets for a man I don't know. And so far, all I know about you is that Sheriff Nolan says you're good, and you agree.'

Ryker shrugged. 'Nolan said you wanted to hire a man, ma'am. If you changed your mind, then I'll be going.'

'I've not changed my mind.' Her voice was cold. 'I'm offering five thousand dollars for the men who killed my husband.'

'Nolan said there was only one man.'

She shrugged: 'Gunmen are hired, Mister Ryker. You should know that. I want the man who shot my husband because he will point to the man who hired him. Five thousand should cover both, I think.'

'Depends.' Ryker began to wonder if she was hiring or just talking. 'On how difficult it is. Where he is. Things like that.'

'But you are interested?' She rose from the chair, smoothing the folds of her dress. 'Are you not?'

'Sure.' Five thousand was plenty of dollars. 'I'm interested.'

'Then show me how good you are.' Her smile challenged him. 'I'll not take just your word.'

A hard core of anger burst in Ryker's mind: he knew he was good. One of the best. And he wasn't accustomed to having his skills questioned by a woman.

'Come with me.' He turned and went out of the room, not waiting to see if she followed. Her footsteps told him that she was as he strode through the saloon and hauled the big Sharps from the saddle bucket. Spun round so that she jumped clear of the batwings as he pushed back inside and paced to the rear door.

She followed him out on to the empty ground that bled into the wasteland behind the *What Cheer*.

Ryker picked up a wooden crate filled with empty bottles.

Paced out three hundred long steps, and set the

bottles on the ground. There were nine of them, and he dug each one firmly into the dry soil before going back to the rear stoop of the saloon.

He cocked the Sharps and raised the heavy carbine to his shoulder. The air was still as he sighted on the bottle furthest to the left and fired.

The .50 calibre slug shattered the neck, spraying fragments of glass in a thin arc beyond.

Ryker reloaded and fired again. The second bottle was reduced by the length of its neck.

He loaded afresh and began to fire automatically. Concentrating on speed. When he was finished, all nine bottles were broken down to the shoulder.

'Target shooting.' Laura Tennant's voice was faintly contemptuous. 'I've seen that done at County Fairs.'

Ryker blew gently on the loading gate of the Sharps, clearing it of residual powder. He was getting angry.

'Throw one in the air. High as you can.'

The woman picked up her skirts and stepped down off the porch. He ankles were trim as her waist. She went over to the bottles and gingerly lifted one clear of the dirt.

Ryker cocked the Sharps.

Without waiting for him to call it, she tossed the bottle high above her head.

Ryker swung the buffalo gun up to his shoulder. Trailed the upwards arc of the glittering bottle, and squeezed the trigger. Shards of glass burst like a pale firework over the empty plain.

Ryker levered the spent cartridge clear of the breech. Thumbed in a fresh load and capped the nipple. The woman tossed a second bottle up, and without thinking he sighted and fired.

The bottle exploded.

'You shoot well.' She began to walk back towards him. 'But why use a single-shot? Wouldn't a Winchester be better?'

'Depends.' The gunslinger cradled the Sharps in his folded arms. 'A Winchester'll fire faster, but it's not so accurate. This thing can hit clear on the half mile. Further, if it's sighted right. Way I see it, I can hit a target an' still be out of range. That gives me time to reload while the other feller's still looking for me. Fast fire's mostly useful for close work.'

'And how are you on that?' Again her voice challenged him. 'Can you work up close?'

'I'm alive,' grunted Ryker. 'Hold this.'

He passed her the Sharps and drew his Colt.

The bottles still remaining were way out of range for the handgun, so he pointed at a scrubby cholla jutting from the ground twenty feet away. 'See that?'

She nodded and he began to trigger shots.

Chunks of cactus flew loose, the bullets ploughing a wide hole through the centre.

Ryker grinned, pleased with himself, and began to thumb the ejector rod mounted under the barrel. The spent shells jumped clear of the gate as the rod drove back into the cylinder. The gunslinger emptied the chambers and fetched a handful of shells from his vest pocket. The new cartridges dropped smoothly into the loading gate and he snapped the retaining hinge back in place a good thirty seconds faster than he might have had his old Navy model ready.

That was the difference between the new Peacemaker Colts and the old models. The difference between cap and ball loading, and a pistol that could take ready-made brass cartridges. If he was still using the Colt's Navy he would have needed to thumb a paper cartridge into each cylinder and tamp it down before settling a cap over the nipples of each chamber. And then – to be sure of avoiding flash fire – he would have needed to grease each chamber-front before inserting the next shell.

The new gun with its new loads was a faster weapon. Not quite so accurate, perhaps, but far sturdier and far easier to load. He was glad to have won a pair.*

'Target shooting again.' Laura Tennant's voice held less of a sneer now, but it was still doubtful. 'I thought gunmen could fire from the hip.'

Ryker holstered the pistol, struggling to contain his irritation.

'Sensible man sights in first, ma'am. He picks his target and makes sure he hits it. Any other way, you just waste bullets when one'll do. Man only draws off the hip when he don't have another choice.'

'The man I hire might not have any choices.' She smiled, brushing a strand of auburn hair from her face. 'Show me.'

'The cactus?' Ryker nodded at the cholla that was bleeding water from the hole in its centre. 'Fast?'

'If you can.'

'The hell I can!'

He drew as he said it, squeezing down on the trigger as his forefinger closed through the guard. At the same time his thumb dragged the hammer back, so that the pistol cleared the Mexican-loop holster ready to fire, only the faint pressure of his thumb holding it back from detonation.

He let the hammer slip.

A wing of cholla burst loose from the main stem.

He hiked the hammer back and fired again.

And again.

And three times more.

* See *Gunslinger 8 – Peacemaker!*

The hunk of cactus danced over the dirt. Each one of Ryker's bullets threw the pulping fragment further across the prairie. And each new shot hit and flung it further still.

He emptied the gun. Reloaded. And turned to the woman.

'That prove it?'

She smiled: 'I think it does. You're as good as they say, Mister Ryker. I believe I'll hire you.'

'My husband was a surveyor, Mister Ryker. He worked for the Army for a time. When they were locating new forts in the Arizona territory. That was when he found it.'

They were sitting in Laura Tennant's room. She was sipping tea she had brought with her. Ryker was drinking whisky.

'It was purely accidental. He was surveying a new trail when the Apaches attacked. He was with a foreigner. A Russian, or the son of Russian immigrants. The Indians killed the Russian and wounded Matthew. But he managed to get clear, so the Army sent him home.

'He came back to Washington and told me about his find. He said it was the biggest silver vein anyone had ever found. So we . . .'

'How come it's not opened up?' Ryker asked, interrupting.

The woman sipped her tea with disapproving eyes.

'Matthew's companion was dead, Mister Ryker. Matthew himself was badly wounded. All his notes were lost. No one knew about the vein, except Matthew.'

'Not you?' Ryker emptied his glass and poured another. 'He didn't tell you?'

'No.' She shook her head. 'He always claimed that

women were bad for business. He kept the knowledge to himself – at least, the exact knowledge of the location. He realised he would need help to exploit the strike properly: he didn't want to start a rush.'

'Felt like keeping it to himself?' Ryker grinned. 'More money that way?'

'Himself and three others.' The woman ignored his jibe. 'He came from a family nearly as good as mine. That gave him connections, so he found three partners. Men with sufficient money and influence to open up the lode without starting a riot.'

Ryker grinned again, 'Or losing the profits.'

Laura Tennant frowned. 'Men capable of developing it sensibly. Responsible men, who would not let the kind of riff-raff that fouled California flood in.'

'And now he's dead,' said Ryker. 'And you don't know where the silver is.'

'But someone does.' Her lovely face clouded over, lines tracking between her eyes as she frowned again. 'Matthew must have told one of his partners.'

'Why?' Ryker sipped his whisky, asking the question deliberately in order to draw a clear response.

'Why else would anyone hire a man to kill Matthew? It must be one of his partners.'

'Tell me.' Ryker patted the wad of notes on the table. 'You're hiring me to find the man who killed your husband, and it looks like your husband's partners can lead me to him. And the other man.'

'Yes.' She drained her cup and set the leaves tidily in the bowl. Poured a fresh measure, and began to speak in a low voice. 'There are three, as I told you. One is a rancher in Texas. Colby Studenmire. He has a place on the Pecos river. The second is a businessman in Colorado. He lives in Trinidad, and his name is Beaufort Valance. The third is in Kansas City, a riverboat owner. He is called Nathan Wayne.'

'Jesus!' Ryker emptied his glass. 'Your husband sure spread them about.'

'Five thousand dollars must surely cover a lot of territory, Mister Ryker.' Her eyes were hooded as she lifted her cup. 'Will you do it? Or shall I find someone else?'

'No.' Ryker shook his head. 'I'll take it. Give me the names on paper and I'll start tomorrow.'

'We, Mister Ryker.' She put down her cup. '*We'll* start.'

Ryker was suddenly confused. He had thought the woman would remain in Tucson until he found the killer and the man who had hired him.

'We?' he asked. 'Where's the *we* come from?'

'Here.' Laura Tennant patted the valise from which she had drawn the notes in front of the gunslinger. 'I want to be there when you find Matthew's killer.'

Chapter Four

Ryker bought tickets on the eastbound stage that ran through Tucson from California, continuing on across Arizona into New Mexico and Texas. The route ended in San Antonio, but he planned to disembark at a township called Bayard. Studenmire's ranch was a day's ride north.

When the Concord pulled in to the depot the gunslinger hitched his big black horse behind and slung his saddle on top. Laura Tennant appeared dressed in dark brown travelling clothes, with a sweating Chinaman humping two heavy cases behind her.

'It'll be a long ride.' He still hoped to put her off coming with him. 'Won't be easy, neither.'

'I can take it.' She smiled demurely; infuriatingly. 'Please don't worry about me, Mister Ryker.'

The gunslinger shrugged. He felt less and less like worrying about her: Laura Tennant was the kind of woman who could look after herself.

He opened the door and handed her up the fold-down steps. A drummer in a grey suit, with a curly-brimmed derby settled on his dark hair, helped her inside. Ryker turned away to check his horse.

'How long you figger to be gone?'

Nolan ambled forwards, his damaged arm resting over the swell of his belly. The sling was even more stained now, the original white lost under the rainbow coloration of spilled food. It smelled faintly of chilli.

'Be a few months, I guess.' Ryker grinned ruefully. 'Texas, Colorado, Missouri. That'll take a while.'

'Yeh.' Nolan touched his wounded arm. 'Get paper when you find him, Jack. Most likely be a reward on him.'

'How much you figure your arm's worth?' asked Ryker.

'To me? Or the county?' Nolan snorted. 'That bastard shot me in my eatin' arm. That's worth plenty.'

Ryker chuckled: 'Maybe you'll lose some weight.'

'All aboard!' The driver's shout covered the fat lawman's reply. 'Next stop, Tombstone.'

There were four passengers: the woman, Ryker, the drummer, and a cattle buyer, a man of about forty with greying hair and a hard-muscled body under his dark suit. They introduced themselves and then fell into silence as the Concord rolled over the arid scrubland of southern Arizona.

The landscape was mostly flat, broken only by the tall, skeletal shapes of saguarro and the distant bulk of the mountains. The stage made good time, the driver holding the team to a steady canter that ate up the miles between Tucson and the first way-stop.

They reached it at dusk: a low adobe building with a corral and smithy out back. It stood alone in a vast expanse of empty prairie, the gleam of the kerosene lanterns the only points of light other than the stars.

The stage shook to a halt as two men came running out to unhitch the team and replace the tired horses with fresh animals. The passengers and crew climbed down and went inside the shack.

The drummer and the cattle buyer headed straight for the bar. Ryker escorted the woman to a table where jugs of clear spring water were set out. He filled her a glass.

'Thank you.' She used a lacy handkerchief to dab moisture over her face. 'How much longer will it take?'

'To Bayard?' Ryker shrugged. 'Two weeks. Maybe more. Depends on the weather and the road. There could be Indians or bandits. You could always . . .'

'I'm not going back, Mister Ryker.' Her voice was firm. 'I'm coming with you all the way.'

'Your choice, ma'am.' Ryker slapped his hat against his coat to clear the dust of passage. It gusted out and began to settle on the water. 'Now, if you'll excuse me?'

He went outside and loosed the black horse from the coach. Led it over to the water trough and scrubbed the travel sweat from the smooth, glistening flanks. The stallion snickered gratefully as he fed it oats.

When he went back into the way-station there was food on the table. Stew and potatoes, washed down with coffee. He was halfway through his plate when the driver and guard stood up and shouted for the passengers to get inside the coach. Ryker grabbed a hunk of bread and dipped it deep into the stew, chewing as he climbed into the Concord.

Twighlight had turned into full darkness, and the prairie was lit by the ethereal radiance of a waxing moon. The rutted trail shone bright before the stage coach, shadows rendering the ground deceptive as the fierce glow of the sun. By common consent the passengers hauled down the blinds and went to sleep as best they could.

Ryker slept easily, accustomed to taking what rest was available under whatever circumstances. He did not enjoy using a stage, but accepted the necessity when it was inevitable. Settling back against the worn leather fittings he slanted his hat over his face and braced his long legs against the opposite seat. His thumbs were hooked into the topside of his gunbelt, the fingers of his right hand curled lazily around the butt of his Colt.

Beside him, Laura Tennant removed her bonnet and settled her head against the faded upholstery. After a while her eyes closed and her head lolled to the side. It came to rest on Ryker's shoulder. Started up. Then lolled back, auburn hair tickling his jaw. He smoothed it down, and the woman sighed, leaning her full weight against him.

She smelled of warmth and perfume. Her clothes gave off a faint odour of sweat that mingled with the scent she had applied to her body and the clean, fresh odour of her hair. Ryker eased his left arm clear of the seat and draped it around her shoulder. The woman sighed and tucked herself into the angle of his arm. Slowly, as though in a dream, she turned sideways, adjusting her body so that it rested across the seat. Her head slid down until it rested on Ryker's thighs. The gunslinger crossed his boots so that the woman's head was settled comfortably in the cup of his legs.

His right hand was still free to draw his gun.

And the stage rolled on.

It rolled through a clear, star-lit night. To east and west the lines of the Mogallons and the Dragoons reflected back the glitter of the sky. Nightlight danced along the rimrock like fairy fire, all silvery and evanescent where it reflected from the bare stone and the Spring-shiny leaves of the trees. Where it reflected from the frosted grass and the distant streams.

The trail was smooth enough that the Concord rolled gently as a ship on a placid sea, the steady rhythm of the horses' hooves forming a soothing counterpoint to the creak of harness.

Ryker slept.

Their next stop was at dawn. Just long enough to eat breakfast and change the team before pushing on.

A day later they reached El Paso.

The drummer and the cattle buyer got off there, fading into the early mist that surrounded the sprawling cow town already loud with the bellowing of cows and the deeper roaring of bulls.

The stage waited over a full day, during which time both Ryker and the woman took the opportunity to bathe and change their clothes. The lay-over was good for Ryker's horse. The animal had paced the stage all the way from Tucson, and though it had not been hauling any more than its own weight, it was still getting tired. The day's rest brought it back to full strength.

Soon after dawn they moved on, accompanied by two new passengers. One was a territorial deputy with a fresh-faced kid in tow. The boy had shot a man in a fight over a saloon girl, and now the deputy was taking him to San Antonio.

They seemed more like friends than lawman and prisoner.

And when the Comanches hit, the peace officer unlocked the handcuffs on the youngster's wrists and passed him a Winchester.

They came in from two sides, yelling Indians mounted on painted ponies. They hit from both sides at once, cutting in on the stage in a staggered vee-shape that brought them head-on at the team.

The right-side leader went down with five arrows sprouting from chest and neck. The falling weight dragged the second leader out of line, so that the remaining horses rode into the leaders, tripping on the flailing limbs and crushing the left-hand pony under their panicked weight.

The pole of the stage went on running as the vehicle forced its momentum through the tangled mass of horseflesh. The driver was hauled clear of the box as the reins wrapped tight about his right wrist snapped him from the seat.

He screamed, a long, wailing cry that ended as he fell amongst the horses and choked on the hooves that crushed his skull and chest.

The pole caught on the flank of a horse. Drove through, so that the animal screamed and got pinned to the ground as the wood dug out its guts and embedded in the sand.

The coach lurched, pivoting on the apex of the pole. And spun over, turning on its side.

The upended guard fired both barrels of his shotgun as he pitched clear of the box.

A swathe of ten-gauge shot blasted two Comanches clear of their pad saddles, then a third rode in close and plucked the guard up on the point of his lance, whooping as the stone tip emerged from the man's back in a welter of blood.

The Concord hurtled upright, then pivoted over to crash down on its side. Laura Tennant screamed. The marshal and the kid struggled to get clear of the overturned coach.

Ryker put a foot on the woman's ribs and punched the topside door open.

He hauled himself out with the Colt cocked and ready.

A Comanche rode in close, bow drawn back to loose an arrow at the gunslinger's face.

Ryker squeezed off a shot as the shaft left the bow.

Bullet and arrow hit together. The wooden shaft embedded in the side of the coach, an inch from the gunslinger's face. The bullet hit the Comanche dead centre of the chest. It burst in through his quill breastplate and pulped his left lung before exiting from his back with sufficient force to lift him from his saddle and hurl him against the next rider. His corpse tumbled across the mustang's neck, bringing it down.

Living horseman tangled with the dead. Ryker powered clear of the overturned coach, firing as he fell. The second Indian screamed as the shot plucked through his ribs and pitched him away from his terrified pony.

The marshal and the youngster came out from the Concord.

The lawman was firing a pair of Navy Colts, the cylinders worked over to handle ready-made shells. The kid was using the Winchester.

They were both good. They downed nine Comanches between them before an arrow plucked through the lawman's right eye, the tip emerging from the rear of his skull. The kid shot the rider and grabbed up the two handguns as his carbine emptied.

He came up on his feet, both guns pointed out and spouting fire, face curved into an ugly snarl. Three more Comanches went down. Then an arrow hit him low down on the left side and a charging horseman seized the opportunity to come in close with a lance angled down for a belly thrust.

The kid got up on his knees and fired at the same time as Ryker. The Indian somersaulted over his pony's haunches with twin streamers of blood spraying from his midriff. And another rider came in to plant a lance in the kid's back.

It went in between his shoulders, the stone tip emerging from the front of his chest. He shouted as the pain hit, spilling forwards on his face as the force of the blow smashed him into the ground. Ryker swung round, levelling the Colt on the Indian's face.

The hammer clicked uselessly on an empty cylinder, and the Comanche whooped, leaving his lance dug into the ground as he tugged a stone-bladed hatchet from his belt.

Ryker dropped the Colt into the holster and swept his hand down to his boot in the same movement. It lifted clear with the Remington derringer he hid there cocked and pointed. The Comanche swept in close, tomahawk raised to cleave the whiteman's skull. Ryker squeezed the trigger. And the .41 calibre ball tore a bloody hole through the Indian's face.

Eyes and nose collapsed into a single orifice that wept bloody tears from the cyclopean gap. The Indian dropped the hatchet, falling backwards over his pony.

Ryker thumbed the second barrel of the tiny pocket gun into the firing position and reached under his coat to haul the second hide-away pistol from its holster on his belt.

Two more Indians came in fast. One carried a bow, the other a Henry carbine.

Ryker stood up, both arms stretched out before him, braced against the kick of the derringers.

The two pistols went off together. And air roiled about his head as .36 calibre ball and flint-tipped arrow whistled by him.

The Comanches hurtled from their ponies, the charging animals creating a double rush of wind as they went by. The riders stretched their lengths in the dust, bloody holes showing on their chests. They kicked around for a while, lungs and hearts fighting to stay alive against the draining holes punched through their bodies by the heavy calibre balls. Then they lay still, only wispy gusts of air disturbing the slowing motions of their bleeding bodies.

Ryker looked round.

Four Indians were still mounted, hanging back out of range of the little handguns.

The gunslinger shifted the barrel of the second derringer and dropped the first back in his boot. Holding the other in his left hand, he drew his Colt.

Thumbed the loading strap open.

The heated cartridges were expanded too wide to slide clear of the gate, so he dropped the derringer into his left side pocket and began to work the ejector rod.

The Indians recognised their advantage and charged forwards.

All four carried lances. And all four poles were angled at Ryker's chest.

Time slowed as adrenalin flooded through the gunslinger's body, allowing him that fractional leisure that grips a man when danger threatens.

He saw the four Indians thunder in, lances drooping to point on his body. Snapped the ejector rod in automatic movement as he turned the cylinder and began to drop fresh loads into the chambers.

The lances came closer.

Behind him the woman screamed.

He settled six shells inside the cylinder.

Snapped the gate shut.

Cocked the hammer.

And fanned the cock-spur curve as the Comanches closed in.

It was not a thing he would normally do. He was too good a shot to need the spread fire that fanning produced: he preferred – as he had told the woman – to sight and then fire on his chosen target. But with four screaming horsemen angling lances at his belly he had little choice: he needed firepower. Fast. And fanning was the only way to achieve the kind of curtain he needed.

Two Indians fell, blood spreading across their chests, from their ponies. The remaining duo rode wide, dragging their mustangs to curving halts behind him before charging back.

He dropped the Colt on the sand and picked up a fallen lance. As the first horseman came in he swung it in a curving arc against the pony's eyes. The mustang screamed as the sharp stone tip cut a weeping gash across its face. It began to buck so that the rider fought to retain control.

Ryker turned the lance, driving it hard against the Comanche's ribs. The head dug in through leather shirt, grating off the ribcage to puncture upwards into the lung.

The Comanche dropped his own lance and clutched both hands around the pole stuck into his ribs. Ryker leaned all his weight on the haft, dragging the man clear of his mount as the running pony came towards him.

He ducked to the side, letting the second warrior go by with wide-open eyes and wider mouth.

The lance grounded on soil. Pivoted as the charging mustang bucked its rider clear. The Comanche screamed, sliding down the length of the pole with his guts trailing behind.

Ryker turned, hauling the derringer from his left pocket.

He slid the barrel of the over-and-under pistol to

the firing stance. Cocked the hammer.

Fired.

Dirt sprayed around his feet as the lance grounded in earth.

The mustang's shoulder hit him, spinning him sideways as the animal plunged by, riderless. For the last Comanche was spread like a wet red blanket on the dirt behind.

Ryker climbed on his feet, reloading his guns with instinctive precision.

He stared at the final Indian, watching the blood pump clear of the man's chest with the casual interest of a professional gunslinger; consumed with his kill.

He worked the spent shells from the chambers of the two derringers and reloaded both guns before sliding the one into his boot holster and the other into the tuckaway at the base of his spine. Then he picked up his Colt and blew the dust clear of the chambers before thumbing fresh loads into all six chambers.

Smoke hung thick around the overturned coach, the acrid stink of the powder hiding the sweeter smell of blood. Ryker glanced round, then holstered the Colt: all the Indians were dead. And so were most of the horses. His own stallion was fretting nervously at the full extent of the drag line. Its ears were flattened back and its eyes were rolling around to show the whites as it squealed its fear and its fury at remaining hitched. Cautiously, wary of the animal's temper, Ryker moved towards it. He took hold of the rope and worked his way along, taking up the slack so that the black's head was gradually forced down to where he could take hold of the bridle.

He spoke softly, gentling the animal, calming it until he was able to remove the drag rope and walk it up to the wrecked Concord.

His saddle was pitched loose of the top-rack. He picked it up and slung it on the horse's back, fastening the girth tight and checking the Sharps before turning towards the stage.

The coach was over on its side, the left-hand front wheel broken and a bristle of arrows jutting from the woodwork. Ryker clambered on to the angle of the seat and peered inside. Laura Tennant was crouched down where the seat met the wall. Her hair was fallen loose from its pins and her generous mouth was set in a determined line. She clutched a tiny Remington-Elliot in both hands, the narrow muzzle angled up at the sky.

'Don't shoot.' Ryker was unpleasantly aware of the damage the miniature pistol could do at close range. 'They're all dead.'

He ducked back, waiting until the faint click of the lowered hammer told him it was safe, then reached down to help the woman clear.

'Oh my God!' She looked round at the corpses. 'What do we do now?'

'Get the hell out of here.' Ryker looked up to where the first buzzards were circling their position. So far there were only three, but more birds were gliding in from the north, marking them as surely as a signpost. 'Before any more Comanche come looking for trouble.'

He went to check the stage team, hoping to find a pony still sufficiently healthy to ride. He was unlucky. Two animals had been killed in the first rush. One more had collected a stray bullet through its belly, and the remaining three were strained too badly to carry weight. Ryker cut them loose from the tangled harness and watched them limp away. Then he shot the wounded animal and turned back to the woman.

'We'll double up. It'll be slow, but it beats walking.'

'What about my clothes?' She pointed at the scattered cases. 'I can't leave them.'

Ryker shrugged. 'You got a plain choice, ma'am. Leave your clothes, or leave your hair.'

'But we can't be far from a town.' She stared wistfully at her luggage. 'Can we?'

Ryker tried to remember the map he had seen back in El Paso. As best he could recall, they were closer to the next way-station than they were to the town. Maybe three days closer.

'Out here it's pretty easy to be far from anywhere,' he murmured. 'Now let's go.'

Before she could argue any more he picked her up and slung her on the saddle. She squealed, mouthing an unladylike curse, then settled her skirts and pointed down at the black valise.

'I must take that, at least. All my papers are in there.'

Ryker lifted the thing, passing it up to her. She clutched it against her bosom like a mother with a child. Ryker took up the reins and began to trudge eastwards.

Chapter Five

The long, hot afternoon offered no shade. The stretch of Texas prairie spread out before Ryker and the woman was about the loneliest piece of country he had ever seen. The ground was flat and dry and empty. The soil was baked a hard yellow-brown, with nothing growing except an occasional spindly cactus. Here and there rocks jutted from the earth, but none tall enough to afford respite from the burning sun.

Ryker stripped off his jacket. Then his vest. He rolled up his shirt sleeves and walked on with sweat plastering the material to his chest and back. The woman, expending less energy, remained cooler, but even so she gradually removed articles of clothing until she sat the horse wearing only a skirt and blouse.

Ryker kept going until the heat threatened to drop him in his tracks, then mounted behind the woman.

Wary of overtaxing the black stallion, he allowed the horse to choose its own pace so that they moved forwards at a walk.

Sweat trickled down the gunslinger's face, salting his eyes and dripping from the angle of his unshaven jaw. Laura Tennant rested against him, her blouse plastered to her body. Beneath the flimsy material she was naked, and as Ryker clutched the black's reins he could feel her breasts pressing softly against his arms. Her auburn hair was slick with perspiration, the heat causing it to emanate a sweet, scented odour that matched the aura of her body.

The situation was curiously erotic, and Ryker was almost glad when dusk descended, forcing him to look for a likely resting place.

It came down with the abruptness usual to desert country. The afternoon turned suddenly quiet, the ground itself seeming to draw in, sucking away the brilliant glare of the sun so that the air was abruptly cooler, the light assuming a transluscent clarity. A stillness gripped the land, in which the regular thudding of the stallion's hooves was the loudest sound. Somewhere, off to the north, a bird began to sing. Then – surprising in that empty waste – a bat fluttered overhead. Behind them the sky turned silvery green and the sun got red, streaming columns of crimson over the heavens.

Darkness fell like a curtain. At one moment the sun was a fiery ball, shining bright red from the west, at the next, a fading ember that disappeared into velvet blue blackness. A thin moon appeared, its light a waxy yellow against the clearer brilliance of the stars. The sweat cooled on their bodies and Ryker felt the woman shiver, her back trembling against his chest.

He pulled the horse to a grateful stop and slid from the saddle.

He was surprised how tired he felt.

The woman came down into his arms with a weary sigh, stumbling as he held her upright, then settling on the sand when he lowered her down.

He unsaddled the horse and wound the reins in a make-shift hobble about the forefeet. Took off his hat and tilted his canteen to spill water into the crown. When the stallion was finished drinking he passed the bottle to the woman.

'Not too much.' His voice was dry and thick with dust. 'I don't know how long it's got to last.'

She swallowed twice, accepting his warning without comment, and passed the canteen back. He dribbled water into his mouth, swilling it round so that parched tongue and dry roof got moist, then allowed himself one long swallow before capping the thing and stowing it back on his saddle.

'Will we make it?'

Her voice was husky. Dry and dusty and sexy. But not afraid.

He shrugged, settling on his heels, choosing his words with the same economy he applied to the water.

'Don't know. Two more days, maybe. Could find a waterhole tomorrow.'

She sighed and fell back on the blanket, eyes closing as sleep took hold. Ryker folded the blanket over her supine form and wadded her coat to form a pillow.

More stars showed and the night air got colder. He pulled on his vest, buttoning the garish brocade over his chest. Then he shucked into his jacket and reached over to his saddle.

The light was just bright enough that he could pick out the finer details of his guns, though he would not have needed it, as he had taught himself to handle them by touch alone a long time ago.

He worked over the Colt first, unloading and then checking each cylinder and the barrel before oiling the hammer and trigger springs. There was little other maintenance needed, for the pistol was designed as a purely functional piece of weaponry, most of the draw-backs applying to the earlier models engineered out. He loaded afresh, checking the shells for dirt before sliding them into the chambers.

Then he cleaned and reloaded the two derringers. The little hideaways needed hot water and soap to guarantee their efficient working, but he made do with cleaning rods and oil taken from the kit he always carried with him. He scrubbed the powder burns from the tubes and wiped oil down the short lengths of the rifled barrels. Then applied a drop to the trigger springs and slid two fresh cartridges into each breech.

Finally, he checked over the Sharps.

The big buffalo gun was mostly clean, its only discord stemming from the dust that had gathered during the long ride into Texas. Ryker wiped that away with an oily rag, then checked the hammer and trigger mechanisms and loaded a fresh shell into the plate-breech. He set a new cap over the nipple and slid the carbine back inside the saddle sheath: the oiled leather would protect it better than a blanket.

Then, satisfied with his defences, he spread his groundsheet over the sand and went to sleep.

Morning brought back the heat. The sky was a dull grey when Ryker awoke, the night-cooled sands giving off a cool, moist vapour as the first blast of heat struck the land. Layers of red tinged through the grey, shading into yellow as the early sun forced through the mist.

Soon – too soon – the cool greyness was gone, replaced by a clear azure sky that showed no sign of cloud. No colour at all, other than the incandescent globe of the sun.

Ryker climbed to his feet and saddled the horse. Woke the still-sleeping woman, and passed her the canteen.

She had sense enough to take only a brief gulp,

wetting her face on the dew-moistened blanket before climbing astride the horse. Ryker took up the reins and began to plod forwards again, unspeaking as he concentrated on following the tracks left by earlier stages.

The farther they travelled, the hotter the day became. The last vestiges of moisture got burned up from the ground, leaving the sand like the warm side of a griddle. Ryker could feel the heat burning up through the soles of his boots. Felt it burning down out of the sky as his vision blurred with the constant trickle of sweat along cheeks and forehead. He tasted it in his mouth: thin and salty, adding to his thirst.

He walked like an automaton: one foot got pushed out in front, landed, was followed by the swing of his rearward leg. Time and time again. One after the other. Step by step, with the black stallion plodding behind him, the woman slumped loose on the saddle.

Some time around mid-morning he fell down.

He didn't know he was on the ground until the woman's arms tucked under his chest and turned him over far enough that she was able to dribble water into his mouth.

He licked his lips. Tasting blisters. And said, 'No. Save it.'

'You'll die.' Her voice was a croak. Like a raven's cry. 'We'll both die.'

'No.' He got up on his feet and gathered the reins into his burning hands. 'We'll not die.'

She followed him as he stumbled forwards again.

The sand was silent. The heat seemed to suck the noise of the horse's hooves away into the vacuum of the air so that they moved through a weird, dream-like stillness. Once – he couldn't remember how long ago – Ryker had visited a foundry. The heat from the furnaces had seemed to draw all life from the air, leaving behind only a dry, airless *nothing*.

The desert felt the same. Except that in the foundry there had been barrels of clear water with cups chained to the sides, and the workers there had gone regularly to drink, or soak their bandanas, tipping whole – wonderful – cupfuls of glistening, cool water over their bodies.

He began to think about water. Began to see it in the dry ruts cut through the parched land along the stage line he was following.

It seemed that the twin tracks were puddled with muddy liquid. Then the moisture cleared, becoming blue and cool and tempting. The hoof prints left by the stage teams seemed to fill with sun-glistened water: whole mouthfuls of liquid that shimmered in the light.

He shook his head. Shook away the illusion. And cut two strips of leather from the reins, passing one up to the woman.

'Chew it'. Even to his own ears, his voice was harsh, burned-out. 'Give you moisture.'

Without waiting for a reply he stuck the second piece in his own mouth and began to chew automatically as he plodded on.

The leather gave no direct relief, but the action of chewing it released what little residual moisture had stayed contained in their tongues and mouths. Or gave the belief that it did. Either way, it saw them through to noon.

By then Ryker could feel the heat burning up through the soles of his boots. Could feel the salt sweat scraping his shirt against his body. And knew that he couldn't go on much longer.

He called a halt when he saw a clump of scraggy cholla, and draped his groundsheet from the cactus plants to form a tiny patch of shade.

Laura Tennant climbed under with the grateful willingness of a woman at the end of her resources. Ryker poured the last of the water into his hat and fed it to the black stallion, then crawled inside himself.

They stayed as far apart as the shaded area allowed them, anxious to avoid the body heat emanating from their clothes and skin. After a while Ryker went to sleep, exhausted by the long hours of walking.

Shadows woke him, dipping deeper across the heated canvas of the groundsheet than the sun would allow. He turned sideways, cupping a hand around the butt of the Colt.

'Take it easy, feller. We're friendly.'

He twisted upright, seeing horses and men.

Held the Colt back on full cock.

'Feisty traveller, ain't he?' The voice was raucous with laughter. 'Half-dead an' still tryin'.'

'Lay off, Strother.' The first voice was commanding as Ryker eased clear of the shade. 'Poor bastard's near gone with thirst.'

Ryker stood up, looking at a tall man mounted on a tall pony.

Looked round at the five other riders.

They were all Americans. Cowboys, by the cut of their clothes and the horses they rode. And one was holding out a canteen.

He took it. And drank carefully. Wetting his mouth and letting only so much as was necessary slip into his belly.

'Thanks.' His voice sounded better with the liquid wetting the parched cords. Not much; but still, better. 'My horse.'

'First to drink.' The tall man grinned. 'Didn't need much. Seemed like you'd taken care of him.' He shrugged, passing the canteen back to Ryker. 'Man needs to tend his horse out here. He's dead, else.'

'Yeah.' Ryker took the water and ducked back inside the shelter.

He poured some over the woman's face, waking her up.

Her mouth opened before her eyes, sucking hungrily on the moisture. Then her eyes flicked clear of the salt-rimed lashes and stared at his face.

'Water?'

She reached for the canteen. Ryker let her drink twice, then pulled the bottle away. She sighed, savouring the dampness. Ryker fed her more, in little dribbles. She took them gratefully. Then asked:

'Where did it come from?'

Ryker eased her clear of the makeshift tent, and she gasped as she saw the horsemen.

'No trouble, ma'am.' It was the tall man who spoke. 'We all work for the Big S. Colby Studenmire's ranch.'

The only boundary of the Studenmire spread was the invisible line between where the cattle were grazed and where they weren't. The only announcement of the ranch was a solitary gatepost with a headboard burned out in the shape of a massive S.

From that point a well-worn trail rolled through greener country than Ryker had seen in the last few weeks up to a two-storey building that spread along the crest of a hill like a fort commanding the surrounding ground.

In from the gate the trail led up to a ten-foot fence, punctuated at intervals by solid-looking guard-posts of adobe and wood. To one side of the main entrance there was a watch-tower built up a good twenty feet above the ground. One man stood there, scanning the slope below with a telescope.

Two men manned the gate.

Beyond, the trail climbed up higher towards the ranch-house. A hundred yards in it was broken by a secondary wall of adobe, around five feet high, with a wide wooden gate and two more men mounting guard.

By the time Ryker and Laura Tennant reached the main building they had learned that the tall man was Studenmire's ramrod, and that his name was Luke Carlsen. Beyond that, he didn't speak much.

Studenmire was a tall, fat man. Head empty of all but a fringe of hair that draped over his ears the same way his belly hung over his belt. His face was deeply tanned, and his hands were small, accounting for the specially-built Colt he wore, cross-hung on his waist.

Ryker noticed the gun at the same time as he noticed the man's figure: they both gave an indication of his character.

Studenmire was fat with gristle. His weight came from the excess of good living that had followed lean years. His movements were still precise, almost dainty, and the underslung pistol still looked workable.

It was a Remington Cavalry model of 1858, but brass cartridges on the belt indicated that the handgun had been converted from cap and ball loads to ready-fire shells. And the grip was cut down.

Ryker liked that: he liked any man with the sense to accommodate a gun to his personal use.

'Found them over to the west, boss.' Carlsen dismounted in front of the high stoop. 'Got shot up by Comanch'. Feller's called Ryker. The lady's a Missus Tennant.'

Studenmire's face lost its blandness as a frown tucked wrinkles into the smooth skin. Then he regained his composure and spread a wide smile over his mouth.

'Mrs Tennant? *The* Mrs Tennant?'

'If you mean the wife of your partner, yes.' She allowed Ryker to help her down from her mount, but her eyes stayed fixed on the rancher. 'I want to talk to you.'

Studenmire went on smiling. 'You must be exhausted, my dear. And your – ' there was a pause – 'companion. Come inside to clean up. Then we'll talk.'

He turned to look down at Carlsen. 'Luke. Please see to the horses. Arrange a place for mister Ryker in the bunkhouse.'

'He's with me,' said the woman. 'Bed him in the house.'

Studenmire shrugged. 'Very well. Come inside. Both of you.'

He set an obscene emphasis on the *both.*

The ranch was built on Mexican lines, tall, wide-shuttered windows letting in whatever cool breezes blew while the walls shut most of the heat outside. The rooms were spacious, tiled and boarded, with plain furniture and a minimum of drapery.

Ryker followed a Mexican houseboy to a cool, dark room. Accepted the pitcher of lemonade that followed and drank it down in three long gulps as he waited for the promised bath.

It came soon after, and he wallowed in the tub with all the enjoyment of a man too long deprived of water.

By the time he emerged his clothes had been cleaned and pressed, and he climbed into a suit and fresh-smelling shirt that did as much for him as the bath.

When he went downstairs, Studenmire was sipping a drink by the fireplace.

'What is your connection with Mrs Tennant?' asked the rancher, pouring the gunslinger a drink. 'Have you replaced her husband?'

Ryker shrugged, confused by the curious statement.

'Her husband got shot,' he said. 'She hired me to find his killer.'

'And she suspects I might be the culprit?' Studenmire chuckled. 'How ridiculous.'

'Why?' asked Ryker. 'You stand to gain from his death.'

Studenmire's chuckle grew into a deep-gutted laugh.

'I gain nothing, my friend. I've not seen Matthew in years. And I make enough from this spread to supply my needs. I agreed to invest a little capital in that wild venture of his because we attended school together, and because Matt was always in need of funds. I felt sorry for him. Nothing more.'

'Why?' Ryker asked.

'You never knew Matt?' It was a statement. 'He was wild. Always dreaming of big ideas without ever doing anything about them. That woman of his forced him into the last venture. Got him killed, I shouldn't wonder. From what he wrote me, she was greedy enough.'

'She told me she only knew the names,' said Ryker.

'The names of the three other partners.'

Studenmire spread his hands, spilling liquor over the tiled floor. 'Then she knew more than me. All I ever heard was that Matt had located a silver lode somewhere in Arizona Territory. He told me enough about it to convince me it was worth investing a few thousand, but he never told me where it was. I was hoping the widow knew.'

'You don't sound like you like her,' grunted Ryker. 'Why's that?'

'You ever met those thin-faced Washington women?' said the fat man. 'Prissyn' up over their goddam teacups while they tell each other about dirty Texas cow ranchers and their dirty habits? I went through that when I was selling beef to the Government. They were ready enough to eat the meat I could supply, but they didn't like the way I lived.'

Ryker opened his mouth to ask why, but then a young Mexican came into the room with a platter of tid-bits. He was around sixteen years old, but looked younger. And the wrong side of male. His eyes were soft, accentuated by the rings of make-up on the lashes and lids. A hint of rouge accentuated the planes of his cheeks, and his mouth was reddened. He walked with a sway-hipped gait.

Studenmire watched Ryker's eyes open in surprise. And smiled.

'That's why they didn't like me, Ryker. That's why Laura doesn't like me. It's how Matthew and me got to know one another.'

Ryker emptied his glass and reached for the decanter.

'It shocks you?' Studenmire's voice was challenging. 'We all follow our own inclinations. Personally, I find Laura revolting. But I'd not kill her husband.

Her, maybe.' He picked up a piece of meat and sucked it into his fleshy mouth. 'But not Matthew. He meant too much to me. Once. A long time ago.'

'You fat nancy-dan!' Laura came down the stairs, eyes blazing. 'You goddam corn-holer! Matt loved me, not you. He'd never let a brown-tongue ass-lover like you touch him. Never!'

Ryker turned to face the woman, suddenly remembering the little Remington-Elliot she carried. Studenmire dropped his glass and reached awkwardly for the Remington.

'Leave it!' The gunslinger's voice cracked like a whip through the melodramatic stillness of the room. 'Both of you.'

'That queer bastard killed my husband,' snarled Laura. 'Shoot him! That's what I hired you for.'

Ryker shook his head. 'You hired me to find your husband's killer, ma'am. Not gun down anyone you take a dislike to.'

'Thank God someone has a little sense,' murmured the rancher. 'I think I'll eat in my room. But please help yourselves to everything available.'

He spun round, pushing past the woman as he walked heavily up the stairs. A door thudded shut behind him, followed by the scrape of bolts into latches.

A moment later the young Mexican boy went running up to the balcony and the door opened again.

'You should have killed him.' Laura's voice was harsh. 'I'm sure he was the one who hired that gunman.'

Ryker shrugged, sipping coffee from a silver-chased cup.

'That were so, then why not kill us outright? He

must've known what you looked like. He could've had us both gunned down easy. Could've shot us himself, from the balcony and said I was doing what you asked.'

'I asked you to find Matthew's killer,' said the woman; coldly. 'Not give me sermons.'

'He's not the one.' Ryker settled his cup down into the fancy saucer. 'Not him.'

Laura Tennant made no reply. Just stood up and went over to the stairs.

'I'll be in my room. We'll leave in the morning.'

'Sure.' Ryker nodded, pouring himself a fresh cup of coffee as he wondered about the hate the woman was throwing off. He glanced around the room, noting the silverware shut behind the glass cabinets and the rich cut of the few rugs covering the tiled floor. The place had cost money, and from what little the ramrod had said on the way in, it made money, too. More than enough to keep Studenmire in the style he liked. More than enough to make risking it all on a hired killing too dangerous to chance.

He stood up, pushing back his chair, and headed for his room.

Inside, he bolted the door and settled down to sleep with the two derringers under his pillow and the Colt hung off the bedhead at his right.

Some time during the night he woke up. He wasn't sure why until he heard the soft scraping of bare feet on the balcony outside and the muffled sound of a door closing. Studenmire saying good night to his little friend, he decided. And went back to sleep.

He was awake at dawn, brought back to full consciousness by the internal mechanism governing his rest. It was a knack he had always had: to be able to wake at whatever hour he decided on, regardless of circumstance.

He cleaned up and shaved cold, then wandered down to the main room where Mexican servants were serving breakfast. Most were of the same age as the boy he had seen the previous night.

After a while, Laura Tennant joined him. She appeared anxious to get away, a fact Ryker attributed to the odd circumstances of the ranch and the possibilities it opened on her memory of her husband.

Luke Carlsen came in with his hat in his hand and an expression empty of comment.

'The boss said you might be leavin' this mornin'. He ain't around yet, but if you want to go, I got the stallion an' a buggy ready to drive you far as Bayard.'

'We'll go.' The woman said it while Ryker was still thinking about the journey. 'Now.'

The gunslinger swallowed the last of his coffee and followed her outside.

'Where's Studenmire?' he asked. 'Like to say goodbye.'

'Boss often sleeps late.' Calrsen kept his face blank. 'After a hard day.'

'Yeah.' Ryker climbed into the buggy alongside the woman. 'Tell him thanks.'

'Sure.' Carlsen checked the rope on the black horse and then rode round to the front. 'I'll do that.'

'Let's go,' urged the woman. 'I don't like this place.'

The two cowboys detailed to escort them kicked heels against the flanks of their ponies and took off down the slope. Ryker followed as the woman called for him to make speed.

He felt curiously uneasy, but he couldn't say exactly why.

Chapter Six

Bayard was a sprawl of single-storey buildings spread either side of the stage route. There was nothing to mark it out as different to any other tank town or whistle stop Ryker had seen. It was just as dusty. Just as dry. Just as hot. Just as lonely.

He climbed down from the buggy and helped Laura Tennant into the shade of the sidewalk. A cowboy passed him Nero's reins and climbed into the wagon. Luke Carlsen touched the brim of his stetson.

'Ma'am. Ryker. I'll be gettin' back now. Stage comes through in about a hour. Have a good journey.'

The woman watched the cowboys ride away, then turned to the gunslinger.

'How long will it take them to get back?'

Ryker shrugged, wondering why she was curious about an irrelevant matter. 'Little less than it took us to get here: they'll move faster. Three hours, maybe.

'So we'll be gone before they reach the ranch?'

'If the stage comes in on time.' He couldn't understand why she seemed so concerned. 'What's it matter?'

'It doesn't.' She shook her head, reaching up to pat an errant strand of hair back in place. 'I just want to get out of this awful country.'

'Then we'd best get ourselves some tickets,' grunted Ryker. 'We can take the stage on to San Antonio or Houston. After that, you'd best decide the next move.'

The woman frowned. 'We still have two men to see, mister Ryker. I expect you to honour our agreement.'

'I will,' he said. 'So we'll go to Houston. Pick up the railroad to St Louis, then take a boat up to Kansas City.'

'Excellent.' She smiled for the first time that day. 'Let's buy the tickets.'

Houston was the biggest town Ryker had seen in a long time. It had buildings as high as four storeys, and at least four saloons. There were, according to the man at the stage depot, two good hotels – the kind an unescorted woman might stay in safely – and three more of dubious merit. The streets were wide and often paved; some had street lights. And most were patrolled at night by uniformed constables.

Ryker and the woman booked into a place called the *Texas Pride*, taking rooms on the first floor that looked down over a courtyard with a well at the centre and honeysuckle growing up the sunny walls.

Ryker was intrigued by the intricate system of pipes covering one wall of the bathroom adjoining his room. It seemed that the hotel could provide hot water at any time of day. All he needed do was turn a spigot on the fancy enamelled tub and steaming liquid poured out to drown the spiders and cockroaches that gathered on the bottom.

He spent several hours in the tub, running in more hot water when the first dousing cooled, then turning the second spigot to fill the tub with cold water. He soaped his body and scrubbed at his hair, finally climbing out to towel himself dry with the biggest length of cloth he had used since leaving Richmond.

The thought sobered his enjoyment of the luxury, adding a sombre shadow to his pleasure.

He had been little more than a boy when his parents decided to quit the Southern capital to escape the threat of war. Angus Ryker had been a pacifist. A doctor devoted to healing and the pursuit of peace. He had taken refuge in alcohol as talk of the impending war grew stronger, then made the giant step of moving his family west to the new territories.

Along the way Mary Ryker had died of fever. Years later – after Angus had established a medical practice in Settlement, Arizona, and his son had pursued his enveloping fascination with guns to the extent that he was one of the best-known gunsmiths in the territory – the Civil War had caught up with them. Ryker had sold a man a Derringer.

One of the original models produced by Henry Deringer. He had worked it over until it was in superb condition. Accurate and reliable. Guaranteed to kill within the short range afforded by the tiny barrels.

It had been used to kill Abraham Lincoln. And somehow – prompted by rabid lust for vengeance – vigilantes had succeeded in tracking down the man who sold the pistol to a friend of the killer.

John Wilkes Booth was dead, but the North still howled for revenge. So two men traced Ryker to his smithy in Arizona.

And found him gone.

They found his father instead. And killed him.

In turn, Ryker had hunted his father's murderers. Killed them.

And become a bounty hunter when he discovered that his drunken father had mortgaged everything they owned*.

* See *Gunslinger 1 – The Massacre Trail*

He shrugged off the dark memories as he got dressed. Outside, Houston was lighting up for the night. The sky was still bright, but the glow of street lamps and the kerosene lanterns hung outside the saloons and brothels were beginning to outblaze the setting sun.

He felt hungry and curious.

Laura Tennant had been gone most of the day. Looking for clothes, she had said, to replace those lost on the stage. She hadn't wanted Ryker with her, leaving him to organise their passage on to Missouri.

He had checked out the possibilities and come up with the fastest route to Kansas City: from Houston they could take the Central Texas Railroad as far as New Orleans. Then a river boat could take them north to St Louis, where they could transfer to a second boat that would carry them along the branch line of the Missouri to Kansas City. It would take over a month in all, but it was still the fastest way – given the fact that Ryker intended to bring his horse with him.

He had lost several stallions in the bloody years since he became a bounty hunter, and each new mount had been modelled on its predecessor. All were called Nero, and because he insisted on riding the best mount available, they had cost him a good deal of money.

He was unwilling to give his present animal up. Not while his employer seemed to have so much money to spend.

So he was taking Nero with him. All the way.

He went down the corridor and tapped on the door of the woman's room. There was no answer, so he went down to the lobby and asked the desk clerk if Mrs Tennant had come back yet.

'No, sir.' The clerk shook his head. 'But there were two gentlemen in earlier, asking about you both.'

'Why?' Something prickled the short hairs on Ryker's neck. It was like hunting cougar: like when you know the big cats are prowling, but you don't know where they are. 'They say what they wanted?'

'Nossir.' The brilliantine on the clerk's hair threatened to spray loose. 'Just asked about you. That was all, sir.'

'What you tell them?' Ryker's face got creased up with irritation. 'How much?'

'Nothing! Honestly.' The clerk spread loose strands of hair over the register. 'I never told them your room numbers or anything.'

'What they look like?' Ryker wondered who might have followed him to Houston.

'Like cowboys,' said the clerk. 'One was a tall man with grey hair. The other was shorter. Wore two guns. I think he was called Strother.'

'Thanks.' Ryker passed a dollar across the desk. 'If they come back, you give me warning. Same for Mrs Tennant.'

'Yessir!' The coins disappeared like magic. 'I'll do that, sir. Anything else?'

'Yeah.' Ryker made a fast decision. 'Send a meal up. And a bottle of whisky. When Mrs Tennant comes back, tell her I'm in my room. Tell everyone I'm in my room.'

'Everyone, sir?'

'As asks,' said Ryker. 'Even the two cowboys.'

'As you wish.' The clerk was confused. 'Whatever you say, sir.'

The windows looking over the courtyard had heavy wooden shutters hinged against the walls. Ryker closed them.

There were no windows in the bathroom, but he closed the door and set a chair against it anyway.

Then he checked over his guns, making sure each one was clean and ready to fire smoothly. He rested the Sharps against the wall on the far side of the bed, tucked one derringer under the pillows. Then sat back to wait.

Laura Tennant came first.

Her face was wrinkled with worry, transforming her good looks into a mask of concern. She wore a blue dress, so Ryker knew that she had finished her shopping. Right down to the high-heeled shoes she wore.

'Sit down.' He pointed at the chair set against the bathroom door. 'Keep quiet.'

A knock precluded her answer, and the gunslinger stood up to open the door.

A nervous woman passed him a tray covered with a blue cloth.

He set it on the bed and lifted the cloth away. The rich aroma of steak filled the room. There was a massive tee-bone with hash greens and mashed potatoes, a bowl of corn and a platter of hot biscuits. An apple pie with a jug of cream, and a pot of coffee. And the bottle of whisky.

With two glasses.

He filled both and poured coffee. Then cut into the steak as the woman stared at him and said 'What's going on?'

Ryker grinned, dabbing juice from his mouth, and said: 'Wait.'

They ate in silence.

The steak was finished and the apple pie reduced to a few crumbs hanging in the last wipings of the cream before the next visitor arrived.

Ryker had cleared the plates away and was drinking the last of the coffee, washed down with whisky, when a fist hammered hard against the door.

The gunslinger motioned for the woman to move back into the angle of the wall, where it joined between bathroom and corridor, then stepped forwards.

The Colt was cocked and ready in his hand, angled slightly down to compensate for the muzzle's discharge, as he stepped behind the door and reached over to turn the key.

'It's open.'

There was a pause.

Then: 'Ryker? You in there?'

'Who wants me?' He was trying to place the voice. Found it: Luke Carlsen's, and asked, 'What you want, Luke?'

The reply was three bullets that splintered holes at waist height. Followed by a heel against the lock.

The door jumped inwards and Carlsen came through with a Colt's Army model pumping flame in front and the cowboy called Strother close behind.

Ryker wondered why, but didn't wait to ask. Instead, he shot the ramrod through the belly, then turned his gun on Strother.

The first shot punched into Carlsen's waist just above the pelvic girdle. It tore through his belly and came out the far side after deflecting off a fly rib. The big man screamed and twisted round, doubling up as the pain hit and the woman matched his high-pitched shriek. Her face was covered with sticky fragments of intestines and blood that sprayed loose from the massive wound.

Carlsen went down on his knees, chin resting on

the edge of the bed as the Colt dropped from his hand and he burrowed his fingers tight against the holes in his waist.

Strother turned a double-action Starr in Ryker's direction, and the gunslinger fired again. Without thinking. Working purely on reflex.

The Starr blasted plaster from the wall behind Ryker.

The Colt planted a .45 calibre slug in the cowboy's face. It hit just under his nose, tearing through the upper lip and the rim of gum to glance off the spine and ricochet upwards into the brain. Strother's face got lost in a massively gaping mouth that encompassed his jaw and nose and eyes. Jets of blood erupted from both his ears, and he crashed down sideways, spraying Laura Tennant with jets of crimson.

Ryker went over to Carlsen, and pressed the Colt up against the ramrod's face.

The tall man was on his knees, coughing blood over the bed. His hands were wrapped around both sides of his midriff, and blood was pumping from between his clutching fingers.

'Why?' Ryker demanded. 'Why'd you try it?'

'You know why.' Carlsen's voice was a husky mumble interspersed with thick gobbets of lung blood. 'You knew that when you killed Colby.'

Ryker pressed the muzzle of the Colt harder against the ramrod's face. 'I never killed Studenmire. I never even knew he was dead.'

'In his bed.' Carlsen spat more blood over the stained sheets. 'Him an' little Juan.'

'Why think it was me?' Ryker demanded. 'What reason?'

'Happened while you was there.' Carlsen's voice got fainter as his life pumped out between his fingers and his mouth. 'The woman hired you to kill him.

Why not think it was you?'

Deep down in Ryker's mind an ugly worm of doubt stirred. It churned a bit and threw up fragments of grubby muck that he couldn't quite grasp.

He asked: 'How was he killed? What kind of gun?'

'Only a little one,' groaned Carlsen. 'The kinda pocket gun you fancy gunmen carry.'

Ryker eased the Colt away from the man's face and turned towards the woman. He opened his mouth to ask her a question, but then the door flew wide and three men erupted into the room.

Laura Tennant screamed afresh and triggered the little Remington-Eliott she had taken out of her poke bag.

The .22 slug hit Luke Carlsen in the left temple.

It was a tiny bullet, but enough to puncture the fragile bone covering the left side of his brain. The ramrod grunted, his head jerking sideways as a little red hole appeared just over his ear. His hands fell loose from his stomach, allowing twin trickles of red to pulse down over his hips as a separate runnel gouted from the side of his skull.

'What in the hell's going on here?' The speaker was broad-gutted. Carried a shotgun with both barrels sawed down to around ten inches. And wore a star pinned to his shirt.

Laura burst into tears.

Ryker put his Colt down carefully on the floor.

'Best you both came down an' talk in my office,' said the lawman. 'Now.'

Chapter Seven

Ryker clutched the bars with hands knuckled white with rage. His handsome features were set in a furious mask, the rising blood darkening his tan so that his face grew black with the barely-contained anger. He stared out at the lawman carefully itemising his property with the aid of a grinning deputy.

'One Sharps buffler gun.'

'Check.'

'One o' them new Colts.'

'Check.'

'Pair o' hideaways. Derringers.'

'Remingtons.' Ryker corrected automatically. 'Only reason folks call them that is because Henry Derringer produced the first models. Those are made by Remington. Forty-one calibre, with an over-and-under action.'

'Knows a lot about guns, don't he, Brett?' The marshal chuckled. 'Got all the kit, too.'

'Real fancy gunslinger if you ask me, Mort.' The deputy studied the little pistols. 'Tooled up like a one-man army. An' these little killers are worked over so they load faster.'

'Goddam it!' Ryker's temper got close to bursting point, the fact that he could do nothing serving only to enrage him further. 'I told you! I was a gunsmith. I make guns.'

'An' use 'em.' The marshal's voice got cold. 'On

them two cowboys, fer instance. Funny that Studenmire was shot with a little gun. Just like yours.'

'Christ!' The blasphemy came out through gritted teeth. 'The woman was carrying a derringer. She shot Carlsen with it. A .22 Remington-Eliott. Why ain't she in jail?'

'She was panicked.' The lawman picked up the wad of notes taken from Ryker. 'Two cowboys come burstin' in with guns goin' off. There's a shootin' match, an' then we come in. Like she explained: she was terrified. Thought she was defendin' herself. Feller was dyin' anyway, from that gut shot you put through his belly.' He riffled the paper, turning to stare hard-eyed at the gunslinger. 'I reckon you got paid to kill Studenmire. How else you account fer the evidence.'

Ryker's hands clenched tighter on the bars.

'What goddam evidence?' he snarled.

The lawman shrugged. 'You're carryin' more dollars than I'll see in a few years, feller. You went to Studenmire's ranch an' left after the corn-holer – the deceased – was shot. He was shot with a gun like you use. Then you shot two of his cowboys.'

'They were shooting at me,' rasped the gunslinger. 'I wasn't about to preach at them.'

'Fact remains that three men are dead. Four if you count the Mex. An' you're carryin' too much money to be healthy.'

'The woman hired me.' Ryker was getting tired of saying it. 'Her husband was shot in Tucson and she hired me to find the killer. Sheriff Nolan will back that.'

'I sent word.' The peace officer went on ticking off the possessions. 'Guess we'll just hafta hold you until we hear.'

'That'll take weeks.' Ryker slammed a boot against

the bars. 'A month or more.'

'We all got problems, feller. I gotta feed you all that time. Longer, even, on account of the circuit judge not bein' around fer at least two months.'

'Oh shit!' Ryker let go the bars and slumped on the narrow bunk. 'Oh, Jesus!'

A week passed in boredom and mounting resentment. He was fed three times a day – with cheap food, because the lawman refused to let him use his own money, claiming it was needed as evidence. So he mostly went to sleep hungry, wondering why Laura Tennant had paid him five thousand dollars and then cut loose with no apparent attempt to recoup her investment

He wondered exactly what game the woman was playing, running through the events of the past weeks in his mind until he decided there was no way he would ever discover the truth without confronting the woman. And that didn't seem a likely prospect: she appeared to be gone, leaving Ryker in the ten-foot cell with nothing to do but wait for the circuit judge.

Until the Sunday of the second week.

The Saturday drunks had been cleared from the adjoining cages and the floors scrubbed down with lye and water. Ryker's bedding had been changed and a clean slop bucket placed inside his cell. The place smelled almost fresh.

The deputies had been working double shifts for the last two days, and Sunday – at least from noon onwards – was generally regarded as a rest day. The marshal had disappeared and only one deputy manned the office, sipping coffee with his boot heels grinding marks into the surface of the desk. It was hot inside the cell and Ryker was stretched on the bunk, watching a fly buzz steadily closer to the spider's web hung from one corner. The insect hit the intricate network of strands and struggled to break free. Its exertions served only to entangle it further, and after a while its furious buzzing grew fainter. Something dark and swift-moving came out from the shadows where the wall cracked against the ceiling, angulated legs stepping delicately over the needle-fine mesh of the web.

The spider ran towards the source of the sound as the fly's struggles renewed. It paused a moment. And the buzzing ceased. Then the fly was just one more gossamer-wrapped shape and the cell was quiet again.

It reminded Ryker of his own predicament.

There was a faint scraping against the bars covering the rear window.

The gunslinger sat upright, recognising the sound of metal on metal.

He glanced at the deputy. The man had finished his coffee now and was slumped back with his hat tilted down over his face. From somewhere across the city there came the sound of church bells tolling, and the distant murmur of voices raised in a hymn.

Ryker eased his feet to the floor and stood up. His boots made little sound on the stone flags as he cat-footed to the barred window.

The opening was slightly higher than his head, so he was not able to see anything more than a white-gloved hand tapping the twin muzzles of a Remington-Eliott against the bars. Warily, reaching over from the side, he halted the little pistol's steady progress back and forth.

'Ryker?' The voice was a cautious murmur, but he still recognised it as belonging to Laura Tennant. 'That you?'

'Yeah.'

'Thank God!' The pistol was shoved in across the sill. 'I've got your horse outside. I'll come round the front and distract the deputy. When he gets near the cell, use the gun.'

There was the sound of feet on wood. The noise of something falling. A muffled grunt.

Ryker looked at the sleeping deputy. Then at the derringer.

He broke the latch, tugging the minuscule cartridges clear of the breech. They appeared – like the gun itself – to be in working order.

He reloaded and palmed the tiny weapon.

A few minutes later the office door opened. From the front of his cell, Ryker could see Laura Tennant framed in the late afternoon sunlight. She wore a dark brown dress, the skirt divided. Her hair was piled up under a wide-brimmed hat and she carried a quirt in her hand.

The deputy woke with a start and climbed to his feet.

'Ma'am?'

'I want to talk with your prisoner.' Her voice was cool, full of authority. 'It's important.'

'I'm not sure, ma'am. Marshal said to watch him.'

'You can do that while I talk to him.' Her smile was beguiling. Backed up by the rustle of a banknote. 'A few words can't do any harm, can they?'

The smile stayed on her face while the note disappeared inside the deputy's pocket.

'Guess not, ma'am. But I'll have to stay close.'

'I hope so,' she murmured. 'He's a dangerous man. I'd feel safer with you near me.'

The deputy's chest swelled and he made an effort to sling his shoulders back. The woman went over to the cell door, positioning herself to one side with an apprehensive look at the deputy. He hooked his thumbs in his belt and rested his left shoulder against the bars.

'Lady wants to talk to you, Ryker.'

The gunslinger stood up, moving over to the door with the Remington-Eliott hidden under his palm. He positioned himself close to the door, midway between the woman and the deputy.

'What d'you want?'

The woman smiled and shrugged, reaching up to lift her hat clear of her hair. The auburn curls came loose, tumbling about her shoulders. The deputy stared in frank-eyed admiration.

And Ryker thrust the derringer out through the bars, jamming the muzzle tight against the deputy's ribs. The man's gasp drowned the triple click of the hammer.

'It's only a little gun,' grated Ryker, 'just .22 calibre. But from where you're standing that's more than enough.'

The deputy froze.

'Keys.'

'On the hook.'

'Like you.' Ryker turned his head slightly so that he could see them both, and directed his next comment at the woman. 'Fetch them.'

The deputy stayed still and silent as she unlocked the door.

Ryker said, 'Ease his pistol out and set it down.'

She hauled the big Remington Frontier model clear of the leather and placed it gingerly on the floor.

'Now move inside. Slow.'

Ryker held the derringer pointed at the deputy's belly as the man paced sideways along the bars. When he reached the open door, the gunslinger grabbed a fistful of shirt and yanked him inside. As the deputy was dragged forwards, Ryker brought his right knee up. Hard.

The deputy coughed, doubling over with both hands reaching down to cup the source of his pain. Ryker thumbed the hammer of the Remington-Eliott down and used the butt as a bludgeon. He struck the deputy's neck, just over the knob of bone where the spine leaves the shoulderblades. The man's eyes gaped open, then closed. His body went limp, toppling to the floor. Ryker dropped the derringer into his vest and stooped to roll the man over. He tugged the deputy's bandana from his neck and fashioned a knot, stuffing it into the man's mouth before tying the sweaty cloth to form a gag. Then he unfastened the man's belt and lashed his wrists together. Lifted the body onto the bunk and covered it with the blanket.

He slammed the cell door and turned the key.

There was a half-full spittoon in the outer office: he dropped the key inside.

His gunbelt was hung on a peg behind the desk and his weapons were stashed in a cabinet. He loaded the Colt and dropped it inside the holster, then opened his saddlebags to extract loads for the two hideaway pistols, and the big Sharps. Then he broke open the desk where the marshal had locked his money and extracted the wad of notes.

'For God's sake! Hurry!' urged the woman. 'There's a train to New Orleans due to leave in thirty minutes.'

'I got a horse I'm taking with me,' snapped Ryker. 'I ain't leaving him.'

'I've fixed that.' She slapped her quirt irritably against her skirt. 'They were selling your precious horse to pay for your keep. I bought him. I've also bought him passage through, and two tickets for us.

Now can we go?'

'You think of everything, don't you? Ryker grinned with something akin to admiration. 'Real little fixer.'

Laura sighed, angrily. 'It took some fixing, but at least you're out of jail. Unless you're determined to wait for that fat pig of a marshal to come back.'

'Guess not.' Ryker went over to the door. 'Let's go.'

He eased the door open and glanced along the street. It was Sunday-quiet. The church bells were still pealing and the choir was still hymning anthems. A big black mongrel was investigating a mound of horse droppings, but that – and the flies it was disturbing – were the only things moving.

He went out on to the sidewalk, holding the Sharps ready to use.

'The horse is round the back.'

Ryker followed the woman along the alley. Nero was hitched to a fence post, ready-saddled and looking irritable. Ryker was surprised the woman had been able to handle the stallion.

'Come on.' She tugged the reins loose and passed them over. 'That damn' pony is obstinate enough already.'

'He's not used to packing a load.' Ryker indicated the cases strapped over the saddle. 'You must be pretty good to get him carrying those at all.'

'I can handle plenty of things.' The woman set off at a fast walk. 'Horses aren't too different to men. Both need coaxing.'

'Yeah.' Ryker took the reins and began to follow.

The New Orleans train was about ready to leave as they reached the down-slung ramp of the stock car. Ryker had just enough time to haul the saddle and cases loose and then walk the big stallion up the ribbed plank into the nearest stall.

'Let's move it, friend.' The guard was already lifting his whistle as Ryker staggered up the platform to the nearest passenger wagon, laden with gear. 'We don't have too much time.'

'Friend,' grunted Ryker as he slung the luggage on board. 'You don't know how right you are.'

Chapter Eight

The whistle shrilled down the platform and the brakeman's red flag came down. The steam panting from the locomotive's pistons gusted viciously, driving back the few on-lookers, and the screamer mounted on the smoke stack let loose a wailing shriek. The big engine lurched forwards. Couplings clattered and the passengers clutched the edges of their hard wooden seats as the wagon jerked and began to roll out of Houston.

On the rearward observation platform, Ryker braced his legs against the shuddering and hung wide of the retaining wall as he stared back.

He had to admit that the woman had timed her rescue to a nicety, but it was still a pretty desperate gamble. Everything depended on their staying ahead of whatever message got sent up the line: it was only a matter of time before the deputy was discovered and some kind of pursuit mounted. They would probably gain a little more time while the marshal checked the possible avenues of escape. And the railroad was an obvious choice. There had been enough people around to recall their arrival. After all, a man and a woman loading a horse for New Orleans on a quiet Sunday afternoon couldn't be that common a sight. So sooner or later the lawman had to realise they were headed for Louisiana. What he would do next, Ryker wasn't sure.

What he did feel certain about was that some kind of warrant would be issued. That, and the fact that the sooner they quit New Orleans and headed north the safer he would feel. He had steered close to breaking the law more than once, but he had never been wanted. It was a curious feeling, a reversal of his usual situation. He didn't enjoy it.

Once, whilst repairing a Colt Dragoon for a wild kid who gave his name as Hardin, he had got friendly enough to ask why the youngster insisted on buying a spare pistol when his own would be ready in a day.

'Man can always use some back-up,' Hardin had told him. 'Especially if he's crossed a badge-toter. It ain't so important with ordinary folks, but you get on the wrong side of a lawman an' you ain't never safe. They'll maybe turn a blind eye to a lotta things, but when one o' their own's involved – you sleep with one eye open an' a pistol in yore hand.'

Ryker hadn't asked how the kid had crossed the law, but the advice had got stored away in his mind, and years later – when John Wesley Hardin was a name famous throughout the Southwest – he remembered the brief meeting.

He remembered it again now. And cursed the circumstances that had put him in the same position.

The job had seemed straightforward in the beginning. Not easy, but relatively straightforward. Nolan had put him on to the woman, and Nolan's advice was usually sound. The woman had seemed honest enough: a widow anxious to avenge her husband's death, and with three possible leads to his killer.

Now all that was jumbled up in four shootings and a jailbreak.

And Ryker didn't know who was using whom.

It didn't make any kind of sense for Laura Tennant

to hire him to find her husband's killer – and the man behind the shooting – and then murder one of the partners herself. But Carlsen and the marshal back in Houston had both said that Studenmire was shot with a derringer. And Laura Tennant carried a hide-away. And knew how to use it.

If she had planned all along to kill the rancher and set her hired gunman up as culprit, then it didn't make any sense to break him out of jail.

If all she wanted was to wipe out her husband's partners, then it didn't make any sense to pay Ryker five thousand dollars. Nolan must have told her enough about him for her to realise that John W. Ryker was no ordinary hired gun.

None of it made sense.

And there didn't seem to be an awful lot Ryker could do about it.

He was tied to the woman now. Tied, first, by his acceptance of her money and the promise that had gone with it. There were plenty of people ready to brand him a ruthless bounty hunter. A cold-blooded killer. And he was. In the right circumstances. But he still retained a sense of personal honour, so a promise given was a promise kept.

Second, she had saved him from a long wait in jail and the strong possibility of an exit on the wrong end of a rope. He owed her for that, if nothing else.

The trouble was he knew he wouldn't get the answers to his questions from Laura. She'd skirt around them. Or refuse to answer. Or produce some new story.

He didn't like it much, but it seemed like the only way he could unravel the truth and discharge the obligations he felt, was to go along.

All the way to New Orleans and Kansas City. Then west to Trinidad.

Maybe even to the lost lode itself.

Houston faded into the distance behind the rattling train and the spraddle of adobe shacks marking the outskirts gave way to open country.

The land was green. Lush with early grass and the coastal marshes fed by the rivers rising in the northern highlands of Arkansas and the Oklahoma Territory. The railway ran close enough to the deltas bleeding into the Gulf of Mexico that sea birds screamed overhead, shrieking their raucous displeasure at the interruption in their feeding. Rice fields spread from the raised embankment of the line, the surfaces glittering bright as the sun lowered in the sky, the quilt-like pattern broken by the green of water meadows and melon patches. Occasionally there were groves of orange trees, and the tangy odour of lemons. Ryker thought he caught a faint tang of salt, reminding him of the Pacific and California. And a girl.*

The thought carried with it a memory of pain, and he dismissed it, turning back to his immediate problems.

She was sitting inside. Back straight against the slats of the bench. Her hair was gathered up again, tucked under the wide-brimmed hat that matched her outfit. One elbow was lodged on the window ledge, hand cupping her chin as she stared inland.

Ryker went to join her, easing the cases and his saddle across the gap.

'I thought you'd maybe jumped off,' she said, smiling. 'I was wondering.'

He shrugged. 'I owe you. I don't back down on a promise.'

* See *Gunslinger 4 – Fifty Calibre Kill*

'No.' She studied his face. 'I guess you don't. That friend of yours said you were reliable. He said I could trust you.'

'Nolan?' Ryker chuckled at the thought of the overweight lawman selling his expertise. 'I guess I owe him, too.'

'How's that?'

Ryker stared back, noticing that her eyes were flecked with gold. 'The man who shot your husband put a bullet in Nolan's shoulder. He kinda wanted me to pay the man out.'

'Perhaps he can help us.' For the first time, she looked worried. 'I mean, he's a peace officer, isn't he? He could tell that pig in Houston about us. About you.'

'Maybe.' Ryker set his hat on his knee and wiped a kerchief over his face. 'But it's a long way back to Tucson.'

'What do you think will happen? She glanced round, making sure no one else was in earshot. 'Will they send a posse after us?'

'Not fast enough to out-run the train.' The gunslinger put more confidence in his voice than he really felt. 'We'll reach New Orleans before they can get word along, unless they got another train going through. Whatever, I figure we got a good day's head start, and it'll take time to find us in New Orleans. So long as we take the first boat we can for Kansas City we should be clear.'

'Thank God.' She sighed, leaning back against the hard wood. 'I was worried.'

Her eyes closed and Ryker felt suddenly – oddly – protective. It went beyond his obligations. Down to some place he had forgotten still existed.

Or buried deliberately in the nethermost part of his mind.

Down deep, shut off behind walls of carefully – painfully – developed protection. Like ignoring a gunshot wound in the belly, because the acceptance of the pain would be more than a man could bear.

Laura Tennant reminded him at that moment of Emmylou Harknett.

The girl Ryker had planned to marry so long ago. Back in Richmond. Way back before the Civil War. Before the bloody years that followed had helped him build the veneer of indifference.

Emmylou had died. Trapped with a broken leg in the fire that consumed the Southern city as the victorious Union troops marched for the sea. And most of Ryker's hopes had died with her, along with a good deal of what many people would call his humanity. That death alone, as much as the fever-ridden demise of his mother, or the bloody murder of his father, had made Ryker what he was now.

But for an instant his earlier self seemed to peer through the gory veils of the past.

The woman's face, in repose, resembled that of his dead love. Her hair, as the dying sun reflected through the windows of the lurching train, was the same colour. For an instant she appeared as calm, as trusting, as Emmylou. Her mouth was the same wide, full-lipped shape.

She opened her eyes and said, 'What's wrong?'

Ryker shook his head, dispelling the cobwebs of memory. Shaking off the past. Banishing lost dreams to the limbo in which they belonged.

'Nothing.'

'You look like someone just stepped on your grave.'

'I'm not dead yet,' he grunted, turning towards the window. 'It must have been someone else's.'

Outside the sun spread flame over the land. It

bathed the trunks of the cottonwoods and the cypresses in red light, transforming the green of the foliage to a dark, reddish brown. Like dried blood. It danced rays of red and gold in glittering reflections from the water of the rice fields, glancing through the breeze-rippled cane so that the shifting colours took on the aspects of flame.

High overhead a skein of geese cut their arrowhead formation across the sky, and on a weed-slimy marsh pond a pair of ducks rode herd on a line of young.

'It's beautiful.' Again the woman turned her smile on Ryker. 'Isn't it?'

'Yeah.' He nodded, aware of the dangers of becoming personally involved. Aware, too, that he was hungry. 'They got a restaurant car on this thing?'

She went on smiling. But now a hint of coquetry became apparent. 'Don't you appreciate beautiful things, Ryker?'

He shrugged, answering her smile with a straight-lipped stare only slightly removed from a scowl.

'Sure. I appreciate my belly, too.'

'And that comes first?' She accepted the rebuff in good part, though the flirtatious element left her expression. 'Always?'

'Staying alive comes first,' murmured the gunslinger. 'Staying fed's part of that.'

'They connect a restuarant car when we reach Orange.' She turned back to the scenery. 'We should be there soon.'

'Good.' Ryker eased his long legs across the space between the seats and got his shoulders settled comfortably against the backrest. Then he tilted his hat forwards over his face and closed his eyes.

'Orange comin' up in fifteen minutes. You got half a

hour to stretch yore legs. Dinner gets served soon as we pull out.'

The Negro porter yelled from the front end of the passenger car, not bothering to walk through. The door slammed shut behind him and Ryker eased the black hat clear of his face.

'When we stop, I'll go back and check the horse. You step down like everyone else. Move back to the stock car.'

'You think they'll be waiting for us?' Laura Tennant's face creased in a frown. 'What if they are?

'Most likely they're not.' Ryker eased the Colt out and checked the load, dropping a sixth cartridge into the empty chamber. 'I ain't seen telegraph wire so far, but it don't pay to take chances.'

'What's wrong with your pistol?' She watched as he spun the cylinder, listening to the dry whir of the revolving chambers.

'Nothing.' He holstered the gun. 'I generally carry it on an empty hole. Saves me a bullet in the foot if I trip. Then again, if the law is waiting for us, the sixth shot might save me a bullet someplace else.'

The woman went on frowning. 'You didn't answer all my question – what if they are waiting?'

'We run,' grinned the gunslinger. 'I'll bring Nero down and pick you up. After that we just light out. Fast.' He kicked the nearest case. 'With no excess baggage. The horse can carry two for a spell, but not all that shopping.'

Laura nodded. Then reached down to unstrap the leather fastenings buckled around the outside of one case. She snapped the catches open and pulled out the valise Ryker had seen earlier. Setting it carefully on the seat beside her, she fastened the straps again. Then clutched the valise and her poke bag tight against her chest.

'Head towards the rear of the train,' murmured Ryker, 'and get around the brake-van. That way you'll have some cover. Stay low until you see me coming.'

She nodded, and the gunslinger stood up, lifting his saddle and carrying it out to the observation platform. The locomotive howled a greeting to the approaching town, sparks blowing back through the darkening air. Ryker checked the cartridge in the Sharps' breech and the cap set atop the nipple. Then slid the heavy carbine back inside the sheath and waited for the squealing brakes to halt the train.

Before it was fully stopped he tossed the saddle down on to the low platform and jumped after it. Further along the platform, the braid on his uniform shining in the light of the kerosene lanterns, a stationman glanced curiously in his direction. Ryker grinned, lifting the saddle with both hands. That way they were close to the Sharps.

'Best watch it, feller. I seen folks bust both legs on them boards.'

'Want to check my pony.' Ryker breathed a sigh of relief. 'An get this saddle stashed.'

The man shrugged and turned away, helping to drag down the folding ladders connecting the two passenger cars with the platform. Ryker ambled back to the rear of the stock car. Slung the saddle up.

So far, there was no sign of any law.

A grumbling brakeman stepped over the gap between the two boxes and opened the locked door. Ryker peered back along the platform. Saw Laura Tennant walking slowly towards him.

There was still no sign of peace officers or Texas Rangers.

He located Nero's stall and dumped the saddle on

the floor outside. The brakeman had wandered off, mumbling something about the goddam passengers not being able to make up their goddam minds. Ryker checked the forward ventilation window: the platform was still clear of anything resembling law and the woman was level with the car, stretching her arms and looking around.

He raised his eyebrows, ducking his head towards the station office. She mouthed 'No one' and moved out of sight.

The gunslinger hauled the Sharps clear of the scabbard and leant over the high wall of the stall. Nero snickered irritably, but he looked to have plenty of hay and sufficient water.

Ryker decided they were safe. At least for now. And climbed down.

The forward section of the train – the locomotive, fire wagon, and the first passenger car – was being disconnected. After a while it got hauled clear and a little shunt engine came puffing out of a siding with a restaurant car coupled to the front. Gangers hooked the connecting rods to the second passenger wagon and the shunter backed off. Then the locomotive reversed, linking up with the rest of the train. Water was pumping into the boiler and a team of gangers was stacking wood in the firebox.

The engineer sounded the whistle when everything was done, and the porters began ushering the passengers back on board.

Ryker and the woman climbed up the steps and went back to their seats. The gunslinger set the Sharps on the floor beneath, his eyes still fixed on the windows.

'We're safe, I guess.' murmured the woman. 'Aren't we?'

'Looks like it.' Ryker shrugged. 'But I'll start

feeling it when we pull out.'

As though acting on cue the locomotive gave off one last shriek and lurched into motion.

'Thank God.' Laura dabbed her face with a scented handkerchief.

'Yeah,' grinned Ryker. 'Now we can eat.'

Chapter Nine

New Orleans smelled of honeysuckle and chicken gumbo. The houses looked to be all fancy balconies and wrought iron. The people on the streets were the widest selection of types Ryker had ever seen: white Americans and Creoles and Negroes; Orientals and halfbreeds and full-blooded Indians. The air was warm and sweet; almost sickly, as though impregnated with too many rich odours. The women looked the same.

They found a hotel just east of the town's centre, well removed from the railroad and reasonably close to the docks handling river traffic. There was a stable one block down where Ryker settled his horse before cleaning up and escorting Laura to the dining room.

He tapped on her door, grinning his appreciation of the dress she wore. It was dark green, emphasising the colour of her hair and eyes, with a bodice that nipped in her waist and thrust up her breasts. The neckline was cut low, leaving an expanse of creamy flesh that was further accentuated by the piling of her hair.

The only incongruous note was the valise she carried.

'You planning to take that everywhere with you?' He meant it jokingly. 'Or just to dinner?'

'No!' Her expression clouded abruptly and her

arms hugged the battered case tighter. 'I want to put it in the hotel safe.'

'Fine.' Ryker sensed the sudden animosity, realising he had touched unknowingly on some raw nerve. 'Whatever you like.'

'Exactly.' The intimacy that had entered their relationship on the train was gone. 'Whatever *I* like. I am still paying the way, Mister Ryker.'

He shrugged and led the way down the stairs to the lobby.

The desk clerk accepted the valise, and the woman waited until it was deposited in the hotel safe. Then she took Ryker's arm and smiled at him again, leaning forwards so that the enticing vee of her cleavage was directly under his gaze.

'I'm sorry.' She paused, looking up at him from under long lashes. 'What shall I call you? I can't go on with just Ryker.'

'I got christened John W. Ryker,' he said, interested in the view. 'But my friends call me Jack.'

'Mine call me Laura.' She eased away, taking both his hands. 'Shall we be friends? Jack?'

'Why not?' He fought the memories of Emmylou she conjured up. 'Laura?'

'Good.' She took his arm again, letting her body sway closer against him. 'I apologise for my outburst, but the valise has all my papers and money. Everything Matthew and I shared. It's very important to me.'

'Yeah,' he said, taking her inside the dining room with his mind working fast. 'I can understand that.'

They ate one of the best meals Ryker had ever tasted, washed down with two bottles of wine and followed by coffee and several brandies. Laura kept up a steady flow of conversation throughout, filling his glass whenever the attentive waiters proved a little slow, so that the gunslinger accounted for most of the liquor.

By the end of the meal he was feeling a warm glow inside his belly and a pleasant mistiness in his head.

He realised that he was getting drunk and pushed back his chair.

'Let's go.' Even in his own ears, his voice sounded blurred. 'Best make an early start.'

'On what, Jack?' Laura's eyes caught his, then lowered demurely. 'Have you had enough?'

'Yeah.' He stood up. 'For now.'

He came around the table and eased her chair back. She took his arm, leaning close again so that he had to angle his weight over, pressing even closer against her.

They went up the stairs and halted outside Laura's room.

She took out her key and unlocked the door. Then turned to face him, setting her hands on his shoulders.

Ryker swung his arms around her waist, ducking his head to plant his mouth on hers.

Her lips parted, allowing his tongue to probe the recesses of her mouth. It was warm and moist, her lips soft, answering his pressure as a low moan groaned from the back of her throat. Her hands tightened on his shoulders. Crept up to caress the hair curling down his neck, tugging him hard against her. Her body was hot and firm, and Ryker felt the lust stirring in his pants.

Then she was pushing him away, stepping back inside the frame of the door.

He moved to follow her into the room, but she got the door halfway shut and braced one slippered foot against the lower edge.

'I'm sorry, Jack.' Her voice was husky, her lips moist. 'But I can't. Not now. Not until we've found Matthew's killer.'

'That could be months,' grunted Ryker. 'Maybe never.'

'We'll find him, Jack.' She looked into his eyes, tongue licking slowly over her swollen lips. 'And then . . .'

'Then?' he demanded. 'Why not now?'

'I owe my husband's memory that much,' she husked. 'But after . . .'

The promise was left hanging in the air disturbed by the closing door. Ryker heard the key turn in the lock. On the inside.

He took a deep breath, staring at the blank sheet of polished wood, then let it out in a long, slow, shuddering sigh. Only his shoulders slumped as he opened his own door and went inside to splash cold water on his face.

Five minutes later he was in the lobby, asking the clerk the way to the nearest brothel.

The girl wasn't Laura or Emmylou, or anyone else Ryker had known, but she was good. She had dark brown hair that was almost auburn, and a body not yet sagged by over-usage.

And in the morning she brought him breakfast in bed and offered the use of a razor.

He shaved and dressed, and went out into a delta-hot morning with his head back in shape and his perspectives a little more in line.

Rather than return to the hotel he went down to the harbour and checked out the riverboats going up to Kansas City.

There was no direct connection, but a big stern-wheeler called the *Delta Queen* was due to leave at noon, bound for St. Louis. She had space for two more passengers and a horse, and the factor promised Ryker that he would be able to find a second boat there, willing to take him along the Missouri to Kansas City.

He bought the tickets and went to the hotel.

Laura was eating breakfast in the dining room, glaring at Ryker like an angry wife when he walked in.

He showed her the tickets, feeling almost ashamed of the night until she smiled at him, and said:

'I was worried. I didn't know where you'd gone. I thought I'd upset you so much you'd walked out on me.'

Ryker felt suddenly pleased and embarrassed and confused.

'I was buying the tickets,' he said. 'The sooner we leave, the better.'

'Yes.' She lowered her eyes; girlishly. 'Then the sooner it's done.'

The *Delta Queen* eased clear of the wharf with the massive wheel turning at a quarter speed. Once out into the main channel of the Mississippi she picked up, churning a wake of white froth in a wide-spreading vee shape behind her.

A pilot boat rode escort for the first mile or so, then turned away, leaving the big stern-wheeler to thrust her own passage north through the scatter of small craft covering the mile-wide surface of the river.

Ryker spent the first hour with Nero, calming the big black horse as he grew accustomed to the slow rocking of the riverboat and the steady thunder of the engine. Then he went over to the rail, suddenly aware that he was no more used to such travelling than the pony.

At first, he felt queasy, disturbed by the vast expanse of water separating him from land, but then the steady motion of the boat became reassuring, almost restful. The passage of the *Delta Queen* upriver was gentle, virtually imperceptible, except for the sternward wake that frothed the placid surface of the water.

He watched a skiff go by, its sail bellied out by a breeze from the north, and saw a makeshift raft drift past. The thing was little more than a jumble of timber and used barrels, but the three passengers appeared content to drift, with only occasional use of the steering paddle. The grizzled Negro manning the oar grinned at Ryker, and the two kids – one a freckled redhead, the other a blond youngster – waved. Ryker waved back, suddenly enjoying the odd calm the river seemed to bring.

It was like a suspension of time: nothing seemed to matter, because nothing could happen. The *Delta Queen* was travelling in her own limbo, divorced from the real world until she touched shore again at Baton Rouge.

He climbed the walkway to the passenger deck and tapped on the door of Laura's cabin. There was no answer, so he went into his own room and stretched on the bed. The rigours of the night had given him little time to sleep, so he closed his eyes and settled into the soft pillow.

Soon, he was snoring softly.

The journey continued in much the same way all along the eight-hundred-odd miles to St Louis.

They halted at Baton Rouge to take on wood and passengers and livestock. Then again at Natchez,

Vicksburg, Greenville and Helena. The first big stop was Memphis, then Cairo and, finally, St Louis.

In between there was a series of tiny portages where men hired by the company would deliver wood to the riverboat, or offload supplies, but mostly there was nothing except the water and the distant banks of the Mississippi.

Ryker got bored after the first two days.

There was a constant flow of traffic, but it meant nothing to him. Poker, roulette and faro were played from noon onwards in the boat's saloon, but he had no time for roulette and little interest in the chances of faro. He sat in on a few hands of poker, but lost interest when he realised he was playing against professional gamblers who knew as much about the game as he knew about guns. Which meant he was losing when he sat down with them.

He talked with Laura, learning as much as she cared to tell him of her background. None of which brought him any closer to understanding the woman or unravelling the mystery of her determined pursuit.

She had been born in Washington around twenty years before the Civil War – she remained vague about the exact date, but Ryker guessed she was his own age – and known Matthew since they were children. Her parents had been wealthy, her father using family money to invest in munitions and industry, so that when the war ended the family had been rich. She had become engaged to Matthew Tennant at the outbreak of the struggle, during which he had served with the Washington Engineers.

When the peace was signed at Appomattox, Matthew had come home and married her. Then he had alternated a private business with survey work for the government. He had made money, spending months away from their home until both their parents had died, leaving them even more money. Her husband's last commission had been a survey of the Superstition Mountains, with a view to building a military road that would connect the Arizona forts with California.

That was where he had found the silver lode.

And she didn't know where it was located. She was adamant about that. So much so that Ryker gave up asking her and concentrated solely on trying to persuade her into bed.

She was adamant about that, too.

Until her husband's death was avenged, she could not sleep with another man. No matter how much Jack Ryker appealed to her. If that was what he wanted, then he must carry out his promise and wait for the outcome.

Ryker resigned himself to waiting.

He didn't like it because he wasn't used to the situation, but Laura exerted a curious fascination that he found hard to resist.

And besides, he was intrigued by the mysterious valise.

Throughout the long, slow journey up the river the bag was locked in the captain's safe. The woman checked it each day, and however much Ryker probed, all she would say was that it held her money and personal papers.

He was glad to reach St Louis and step on to the more familiar territory of dry ground and saloons.

Nero, too, was glad, proving it by giving Ryker one hard day's riding, the first hour spent bucking and kicking against the constraints of saddle and bridle.

The gunslinger worked the enforced idleness out of the stallion at the cost of aching limbs and ugly bruises. Nero threw him twice before he was able to control the horse, and then it took a long gallop before the ugly-tempered beast got settled back to saddle work.

When he returned to the hotel, Laura had news.

'There's a riverboat due to leave for Kansas City tomorrow,' she said. 'A special boat. It's taking supplies up for the northern forts.'

'So?' Ryker shrugged, anxious for a long, hot bath. 'You get us berths?'

She nodded, eyes sparkling. 'Yes, I did. But that's not the important part.'

'No?' Ryker looked at her, wondering how she was able to mingle such attractiveness with ruthless determination. 'What is?'

'Nathan Wayne is the captain.' Her eyes seemed to glow. With an unholy light. 'He's handling it himself. He'll be on board.'

'Him and a few crewmen,' grunted Ryker. 'What can we do?'

'Jack.' Her voice got soft; sexy. 'You'll think of something.'

Chapter Ten

Nathan Wayne was a bantam of a man, bristling with suppressed aggression like a fighting cock. He was all of five feet three, his short-cropped grey hair covered by a peaked cap that matched his gold-buttoned uniform. He wore a spotless white shirt and a wide black tie with a gold stick-pin holding the big knot in place. White gloves covered his hands as he welcomed his passengers on board, the purity of the linen accenting the vigorous movements he used to indicate berths. A neatly-clipped goatee, the same colour as his hair, stuck out from a jutting chin; his eyes were green, squinted against the sun.

His First Mate stood beside him, dressed in a similar uniform cut about three sizes larger, checking off the passengers on a clipboard.

'Mrs Laura Tennant.' Wayne frowned like a man trying to recall a familiar face. 'Cabin three.'

'Captain.' She ducked her head slightly, not taking her eyes off his face. 'I hope we shall have a pleasant journey.'

'Welcome aboard, ma'am.' His voice was gravelly as his expression. 'It should be a quiet trip.'

She accepted his hand as she stepped over the headboard of the gangplank, passing on to the deck as the Mate checked off the next name.

'John Ryker. Cabin four.'

Wayne ducked his head and said automatically,

'Welcome aboard, Mister Ryker.'

The gunslinger nodded and followed the woman along to the cabins. Wayne's face was reflected in the windows of the dining saloon, turning to watch their progress. Ryker grinned and went inside cabin three.

It was small, but comfortable, designed with the economy necessary to a riverboat. He watched Laura set the valise on the bed sticking out from the wall and check the mattress, then glanced round the other fittings. There was a commode built of rich mahogany, brass studs protruding from the polished wood, set in one corner. Next to it was a wash-stand and a cupboard. An easy chair was fastened to the floor, and either side of the door there were windows looking on to the deck. A fold-down table was pinned against one wall, with shelves built in above.

A deckhand brought in the two cases and Laura tipped him.

He looked at Ryker: 'Where you want yore saddle, mister?'

'I'll show you.' Ryker turned to the woman. 'I'll see you later.'

'Yes, Jack.' She smiled, and began to open her cases.

Ryker went into his own cabin, not bothering to tip the deckhand, and checked it over. It was built exactly the same as the woman's. The inside wall was thick, muffling whatever sound came from the area beyond, but the outer wall and those separating him from the adjoining cabins were thin, affording a clear sound impression of the activity to either side.

He listened for a while to the woman arranging her clothes and the passenger in cabin five opening a bottle, then went to check his horse.

Wayne's boat was called the *Missouri Princess*. She was a side-wheeler, the deck outside the cabin shadowed by the massive frame of painted wood covering the big paddle. Smaller than the *Delta Queen*, she had only the single passenger deck, situated on the water line. Below were the engine rooms, while above was the tall column of the steerage deck. Cargo was stacked fore and aft, with a section at the stern set aside for livestock. Ryker went there to check his horse.

Nero was penned up with a dozen other animals and a pile of chicken crates. The stallion was alternating his attempt to destroy the coops with munching hay. So far he had only managed to splinter one crate.

Ryker calmed him down and went back to his cabin as the high funnel set astern of the captain's eyrie blasted a shrill warning and the paddles lurched into motion. He settled on the bed and began to check over his guns as the *Missouri Princess* shifted out into the stream and began to cleave her way upriver to Kansas City.

At dinner that evening they were invited to join Captain Wayne on the table set at the head of the dining room. They were the only passengers accorded the honour, and the officers and crew who would normally have eaten with the captain were sent to sit amongst the other passengers.

Wayne had changed from his gold-buttoned uniform to a cut-away jacket with a red cummerbund visible at the waist. He wore an upright collar with a black bow tie, and pants that were striped in gold down the outside of the legs.

Ryker noticed the bulge of a pistol tugging out the cloth of the cummerbund on the left side.

A black waiter brought steaks and wine, and for a while they ate in silence.

Wayne was the first to break it.

'Are you Matthew Tennant's wife?'

His voice was softer than it had been on deck, but none of the harshness was gone. It was still like hearing gravel rubbed over sandpaper.

'Widow,' corrected Laura. 'Matthew is dead.'

Wayne's eyebrows shifted a little. 'I didn't know that. What happened?'

'He was murdered.' The woman's voice got flat. 'Shot down in Tucson by a hired killer.'

Wayne forked up a mouthful of peas and chewed for a while, his eyes fixed on Laura's face. Then they switched to Ryker.

'Who's he?' There was no hint of sympathy or regret.

'Mister Ryker is helping me find my husband's murderer, Captain. Was it you?'

Ryker choked on his steak. He dropped his fork as his right hand moved instinctively to the butt of his gun. Inwardly, he cursed the woman, waiting for Wayne to call his men out and pitch him overboard.

The river captain saw his tension and smiled. It was like watching a lizard catch a fly.

'Don't worry, Ryker. I got too much to lose to risk dumping you. It wouldn't be worth it.' He turned back towards the woman. 'No. I didn't have Matt killed.'

The woman raised her eyebrows, scarcely needing to voice the question.

'I knew about the silver,' said Wayne, 'Matt wrote me a letter asking for money. He didn't put it all down on paper – which is about the most sensible thing he done in his life – but he let me know he was on to a real big strike. I knew he was a gambler from the times he used my boats, but I also knew he was a damn' good surveyor. He reckoned he needed some backing to keep the find outta the way of the Army. Five thousand dollars, he said. I got a partnership in return.'

'You gave him the money?' Ryker was surprised. 'Just like that?'

'No.' Wayne chuckled. Like a parrot chewing grits. 'I never got where I am today by trusting people. I sent word that I needed proof. He sent it back.'

'What?'

Laura spoke before Ryker had a chance to open his mouth. Her fork dropped on to the plate and her hand reached out to grasp the stem of the wine glass. It trembled, so that the claret threatened to spill over the rim.

'I'll show you,' said Wayne. And smiled for the first time. 'Later. In my cabin.'

It was larger than the passengers' berths. A double bed occupied one side of the wall and the other was filled with wardrobes. A table was bolted to the floor, with a brass rail preventing the glasses from falling off. Wayne poured brandy from the decanter set in a raised holder at the centre, then went over to a locked cupboard.

'We're thirty miles north of St Louis,' he said, 'and our next stop is Jefferson. If you try anything, you end up in the river. Both of you.'

Ryker shrugged: 'I'm not planning to kill you.'

Wayne chuckled and opened the cupboard: 'Then sit down.'

They both sat.

The river captain fetched a metal box out and set it on the table. Then he reached inside his fancy coat to produce a key.

Unlocked the box.

And set a nugget of pure silver beside it.

'That's what Matt sent me,' he laughed. 'One hunk of money. Be worth around a hundred dollars if I cashed it.'

'Why didn't you?' Ryker asked. 'Why sit on it?'

'You stupid?' grunted Wayne. 'I never got where I am now cashing assets too early. Makes more sense to wait for the big profit. And that was Matt's promise. He even sent me a bit of map to prove it.'

'A map?' Laura's voice was tense with excitement. 'I never saw a map.'

'Nor shall you, ma'am.' Wayne bowed with a sarcastic grin. 'All I have is a fragment. After all, the nugget might come from anywhere. I argued that, so Matt sent me a piece of the map; that was all. But that piece stays my property until we find the lode.'

'*We?*' Laura demanded. 'I was his wife.'

'And I was one of his partners,' said Wayne. 'I put five thousand dollars into the venture, and I like to get my money back. After all, I didn't get where I am now by wasting money. That's why I couldn't be the man who killed Matt: I'd lose too much.'

Ryker emptied his glass and said, 'He's right, Laura. It wouldn't make sense for him to kill your husband. Not without knowing where the silver is.'

Wayne chuckled some more and set the nugget back in the box, then relocked the cupboard.

'Your hired gunman has sense, ma'am.' He drained his glass and pointed at the door. 'But now I must ask you both to excuse me. I still have a boat to run, and I didn't get where I am without paying attention to details.'

Back in Laura's cabin Ryker said, 'He can't be the one. If he had all the map, then he'd be out looking for the silver. Studenmire didn't know where it was, either. So that just leaves the third man.'

The woman stood up and turned to face him. She set both hands on his shoulders and leaned close against his face. She was wearing a light brown dress with a bodice that was frilled around the cuffs and the line of the cleavage.

The upper mounds of her breasts touched his face. They gave off a scent of something Ryker couldn't identify.

'Dear Jack.' She lifted her left hand to the back of his neck, pressing his face harder against her body. 'You think too straight. Suppose he was lying?'

Ryker's voice was muffled when he replied: 'No reason why he should. If he knows where the silver is, why act out a game?'

Her right hand stroked his hair, then went away.

There was the popping of opening studs. And Ryker felt the material digging into his face slide away.

He looked up and saw the woman naked to the waist.

She wore no corset under her dress, so her breasts were bare, the brown-tipped mounds pointed towards his mouth.

He reached for her, cupping his hands around her buttocks as he drew her body towards him. He opened his mouth to take one nipple between his lips. Laura moaned, pressing her breasts harder against his face.

Ryker pulled on the dress, sliding it down past her hips so that she stood in a foam of petticoats, naked save for the suspender belt holding up her black stockings. He pushed her out, cupping his hands on her hips, staring at the triangle of dark hair dividing her legs.

'Jack,' she murmured, 'I promised.'

'Like a virgin's,' he said. 'Made to be broken.'

'Oh, God!' She kicked her dress away. 'Get undressed.'

'You're the boss,' Ryker grinned, obeying her command.

She was warm and soft and hard. Ryker kissed her, stroking the fascinating length of her thigh between warm flesh and cooler stocking with mounting excitement. She reached down, taking him in her hand as her breath turned into moaning gasps. He stroked her nipples, listening to her moaning and feeling the rake of her nails over his back, running down to his buttocks as she pulled him over on top of her body.

It had been a long time, and his eyes were closed and his mind filled with pleasure as he entered her. She was warm and soft and everything a woman should be as she matched his urgent thrusting and wrapped her stockinged legs about his hips and drew his mouth down tight against hers. He could feel her breasts against his chest, the nipples hard with desire, and the rake of her nails against his back as she drew him harder and closer to climax.

'Jack! Oh, God! Jack!'

They shuddered together, and Ryker rolled away, knowing vaguely that he had done something wrong. But too spent to care.

'I never meant to do that.' Her voice was a husky murmur in his ear. 'I promised myself I wouldn't. But Jack; God, Jack, I couldn't help myself. Not with you.'

He stretched out on the narrow bed, seeking to hold her against him. But she was gone, her mouth drifting like a butterfly over his body. Fingers walking like sensual spiders down his torso and belly.

He felt her mouth take him in and began to say that he wasn't ready. But by then her lips were stroking him and her tongue was exciting him and he was ready.

He lay back, giving way to pleasure that exploded like rockets into her mouth.

And she swallowed and pulled away. And Ryker sighed, enjoying her touch as she stroked his body and curled against him, her warmth easing him down into sleep. He rested back against the pillows, cupping one arm loosely around her, a smile on his face as the delightful darkness took hold of his mind.

Midnight. Inside the pilot house of the *Missouri Princess* a shaded lantern cast a glow over the instruments. Outside the shuttered windows surrounding the dim-lit steerage cabin, two red lanterns gleamed in the soft night.

Nathan Wayne passed the wheel to his Mate and lit a cigar.

The flicker of his match formed a brief pattern on the glass, then was dimmed as he tossed it into the spittoon set alongside the wheel. The river was quiet, lit with silvery gleaming by the half-formed moon that came and went behind the scuddering of clouds. The captain's cigar shaped a pinprick counterpoint to the external glow.

He puffed smoke across the cabin and opened the door.

There was a bordered ladder stretching down from the pilot house to the main deck. Wayne's personal berth was located at the forward end of the boat: a small outhouse built up over the main planking.

He swung down the ladder with the agility of a man long used to manning boats, and paused on the lower deck to listen to the noise still coming from the dining salon. From the sound of it all, he guessed a poker game was in progress, and thought – for a moment – about looking in. Then he decided his crew could take care of any trouble that might erupt, and chose to find his bed: he was due to pilot the craft through the Breaker Shoals at dawn.

He paused for a spell, leaning on the rail as he savoured the cigar and the quiet flow of the river.

Then gasped as something that was simultaneously warm as blood and cold as death slid between his ribs.

The cigar dropped from his mouth.

Sparks sizzled for a moment on the placid water, then were lost in the churning of the port-side wheel.

Wayne felt the hot trickling of blood run down his back and began to turn around.

One hand groped instinctively for the .50 calibre derringer he kept in his waistband. But before he could reach the gun a blade sliced deep over his wrist. It cut through the tendons connecting his fingers to his arm, severing the veins so that his fingers gaped open, filling his palm with the warm wash of pumping blood.

He stared at his hand and opened his mouth to cry out.

Something sharp and cold jammed between his teeth, and he closed his mouth on metal that bit into his tongue and brought a freshing of tears from his eyes.

The same metal grated on his clenched teeth as it was withdrawn. The moon shone briefly on a polished blade that was darkened by the crimson spillings of Wayne's body. Then it was lost as the blade drove in through his shirt and flesh, the needle tip gouging deep into his heart.

Nathan Wayne rumbled once, deep in his throat, the sound driving blood outwards over his lips. And then he was gone.

His feet were lifted clear of the deck so that his body tilted for an instant on the rail, then pitched over. There was a splash that got lost in the greater churning of the wheel, then a momentary pause as the body was picked up by the paddles.

The *Missouri Princess* scarcely lost her motion. Her captain's corpse lifted on one lathe and jammed for an instant against the upward hatching of the wheel-guard. Then it was gone, driven down into the water to emerge yards clear of the riverboat, the dark shape lost in the wake.

No one saw it happen, and no one knew the captain was missing until dawn. By which time his body was miles down stream. And the killer safe in bed.

'Jack! Wake up, Jack!'

Ryker opened his eyes and saw Laura leaning over him.

She was naked, her breasts enticing as they hung above his face. He reached for them.

'No!' She pulled away. 'Not now, Jack. For God's sake, get back to your own cabin. It's almost dawn.'

'Why?' He stretched in the lazy aftermath of sex. 'I'll go back later.'

'Now!' Her voice was urgent. 'If Wayne knows we're sleeping together, he'll know you're more than a hired gun. It's not worth it.'

'That don't make sense,' grumbled Ryker. 'He must've thought something like that last night. And besides, you never complained about my weaponry.'

Laura smiled and kissed him; quickly.

'I had nothing to complain about, darling. But Wayne will, if he knows how close we are. Don't you understand? All he knows right now is that I hired you to help me. If he finds out how much you mean, then he'll think we're working together to take all the silver.'

In the foggy mists of morning it seemed to make sense: Ryker stood up and pulled on his clothes.

The woman passed him his gunbelt and opened the door of her cabin. Ryker shook his head as the cool air hit him, pausing inside the doorway.

'Jack!' Her voice was still urgent. 'Don't forget these.'

He looked down at the package she held out.

It was a small oilcloth bundle, a kind of rectangular envelope with pouches sewn along the inner side. Ryker recognised it instantly as one of the toolkits he kept in his saddlebags.

'Where'd you get that?' he asked. 'I never dropped it.'

'The deckhand, I guess.' Laura shivered in the cool air, drawing her wrap closer about her. 'It must have fallen out when he brought your saddle in.'

Ryker frowned, noticing that the strings were untied. He unrolled the envelope, checking the instruments inside. There was a set of calipers; a bullet mould in .36 calibre and one in .50; a small file; a pair of pliers; a tiny screwdriver; and three scalpels. There should have been four.

'Damn!' He rolled the bundle closed and tied the strings. 'There's a blade missing.'

'I'll look for it later,' suggested Laura. 'Please go now, Jack. I'll see you at breakfast.'

'Yeah.' Ryker nodded, irritated by the loss. The tools were old, mostly geared for work on cap and ball weapons that were now replaced by cartridge-firing guns, but they were still usable. And he hated to lose a tool of any kind.

Laura began to close her cabin door. He accepted the hint and turned away, fumbling for the key to his own berth.

A deckhand passed, face impassive as he said, 'Good night, sir.'

'Yeah.' Ryker grinned. 'It was.'

He got the door open and went inside. Tossing the bundle of tools carelessly on to the chair, he hung his hat and pulled off his boots. Then, still fully clothed, he stretched on the bed and went back to sleep.

He woke two hours later. The river mist was dissipated by the early sun, bright light streaming in past the shutters. He climbed to his feet and stripped off his shirt. He shaved fast, listening to the bell that announced breakfast clanging noisily through the steady roar of the paddlewheels.

The night had made him hungry, and he dressed again quickly, then paced down the deck to the dining salon.

He wondered why two deckhands were stationed outside.

And why they both held billy-sticks.

Chapter Eleven

There was an air of suppressed tension inside the wide room, emphasised by the men posted by the doors and the nervous face of the First Mate. Laura was already at the table, sipping coffee with a worried frown.

Ryker joined her and asked, 'What's going on?'

'Something's happened.' She shrugged. 'I don't know what. They're waiting for all the passengers to arrive.'

The gunslinger poured himself a mug of coffee and studied the other travellers. Two Army officers – presumably in charge of the military supplies – were exchanging low-voiced comments at the nearest table; there were four drummers; a married couple; an elderly woman with a teenaged girl; and three single men who might have been anything from farmers to gamblers. No one spoke much, and those who did kept their voices low.

The Mate checked a list and nodded to the man beside him.

The man murmured something and closed the kitchen door. The Mate fidgeted with his tie, cleared his throat, and rose to his feet.

'Ladies and Gentlemen, your attention please.' His voice was deep, lent a note of high-pitched nervousness by the worry evident on his face. 'My name is Levant. Abel Levant. I am First Mate – no,

Captain – of the *Missouri Princess*. Captain Wayne was killed last night.'

There was a sudden murmur of sound. The old woman gasped and the young bride coughed nervously. Levant raised a hand for silence.

'I say *killed*, because it was obviously not an accident. Captain Wayne was too good a riverman to fall overboard, and there were bloodstains found on deck.'

One of the drummers said, 'Maybe he slipped. Hit his head. He was drinking some last night.' He turned to look at Ryker and Laura. 'With them.'

Levant shook his head. 'Captain Wayne was not drunk. I spoke with him just before it happened: he was sober. Besides, we found this close to the bloodstains.'

He reached down, lifting a length of slender metal that glittered in the sun streaming in through the wide windows. He held it between forefinger and thumb, turning it like an exhibit in a courtroom. It was a flat steel handle, four inches long by a quarter-inch across. A straight-edged blade was fixed to the upper end, about one inch long and honed to razor sharpness.

Ryker set down his cup, feeling a sudden cold grip his entrails: he recognised his missing scalpel.

'There was blood on it when we found it,' continued Levant, 'and the marks on the deck were just a few feet from the captain's cabin. It must have been used on Captain Wayne.'

'Looks like a surgeon's instrument to me,' said one of the Army officers. 'There any doctors on board?'

Levant shook his head. 'No, none.' His forehead got creased as he thought over his next words. 'We shall be in Jefferson by dusk, and the town marshal can be called. Until then no-one is to leave the boat.

We shall be putting in at Montane's Point to pick up wood. The circumstances force me to post guards. Please do not try to leave the boat there, or the crew will be forced to stop you.'

'What about the crew?' The drummer who had spoken earlier looked round at the men on the doors. 'One of them coulda done it.'

'No one will leave the boat,' repeated Levant, 'except the men needed to load the timber. Anyone attempting to leave will be stopped. Anyone.'

He set the scalpel on the table with the distaste of a man handling a scorpion, and whispered something to the man beside him. Ryker noticed that they were both wearing guns for the first time. Navy Colts by the curve of the grips.

'If anyone can help us find the murderer, I would appreciate their coming forward.'

Levant sat down, looking like a man with a bad taste in his mouth. There was a long silence, broken only by the muttered comment of the drummer: 'Jesus!'

The same silence occupied the room while breakfast was served and it was not until the familiar clatter of cutlery on china and the odour of eggs and bacon had filled the salon that people began to speak again.

'I want to talk to you.' Ryker forked up egg, chewing angrily. 'It's time we sorted things out.'

Laura sliced a dainty piece of bacon and lifted it to her mouth. Her eyes were wide; open and innocent.

'You don't think I had anything to do with it, Jack? How could you?'

The gunslinger kept his voice low. 'What the hell else do I think?'

They finished eating in silence, then walked back to the stern of the boat. The cargo area and the stock pen cut them off from the other passengers, affording privacy.

The Missouri stretched behind them, the water calm save for the twin wakes left by the wheels. The banks were lush with oak and cottonwoods, slanting down to the sun-glistened surface of the river in green placidity. A black and white bird skimmed low over the surface, plucking insects from the warm air with a hungry beak.

Ryker hooked one heel on the rail, staring at the woman.

She blushed, staring back.

'Well?' His voice was low and cold and angry. 'What the goddam hell is going on?'

'I don't know!' Her eyes got wide, answering his glare with a hint of tears. 'For God's sake, Jack! Don't you believe me? After last night?'

'Last night Nathan Wayne was killed.' Ryker spat the words, like melon pips. 'He was killed with my scalpel. That makes me pretty goddam high on the list of suspects. What the hell d'you think will happen if someone finds out it was my scalpel?'

'How can they?' She essayed a smile. 'I won't tell them.'

'How come that kit was in your cabin?' He ignored her smile, his own mouth set in a straight, angry line. 'How come all your husband's partners wind up dead soon as you get close?'

'My God!' Her eyes opened wide as her mouth shaped an oval of horror-stricken surprise. 'You think I killed them!'

'Shit! There's not much else left to think.' Ryker hunched his shoulders, hooking both thumbs into his belt. 'We reach Studenmire's spread, and he gets shot in bed. With a derringer. Like you carry in that goddam bag. We get on a riverboat, and Wayne gets sliced with my scalpel. Out of a tool kit you hand me.'

'Jack.' She touched his arm, flinching as he tensed the muscle. 'I was with you all night. How could I have killed Wayne?'

'I don't know,' Ryker allowed, 'but there's too goddam many coincidences.'

Laura sighed. 'It is strange. I know that. But the whole thing is strange. Who had Matthew shot? Surely you don't think I did that, too?'

'No.' Ryker shook his head, still staring at her. 'You couldn't have done that. But you could have hired someone.'

'Jack!' Her face paled, two patches of red showing on the cheeks. 'How can you say such a thing? How dare you?'

'I got jailed on account of Studenmire,' grunted Ryker. 'Now it looks like I could be framed for Wayne.'

'I got you out of jail in Houston.' Her voice was low; trembling on the brink of tears. 'I'm your alibi now.'

'You'll tell the marshal in Jefferson that?' Ryker demanded. 'Tell him we were together all night?'

'If I must.' She smiled again. A nervous, wavery curving of the lips. 'If it's necessary.'

She touched his arm a second time and now Ryker did not pull back. He looked at her, seeing the moistening of tears add lustre to her gold-flecked eyes. She looked very lovely: he remembered the night.

'That still leaves two corpses behind us,' he said; though softer now, less harsh. 'And me wanted in Houston.'

'Perhaps we're being followed.' She moved closer as if seeking protection from the proximity of his body.

'If Wayne had part of Matthew's map, then maybe Valance does, too. Maybe he knew Matthew would be in Tucson and hired that man to kill him so that he could get all the map.'

'Maybe.' The more Ryker thought about it, the more sense it made. Unless he was just looking for reasons to believe. 'It could be that way. But why kill the man with the money? The one who knew where the lode was?'

'I don't know.' She moved closer to the rail, leaning her body against him. 'But if Valance had a piece of the map, then perhaps he thought that killing Matthew would lead him to the other pieces. I never even knew about the map – I thought Matthew had the location in his head.'

'Not in the Superstitions,' grunted Ryker. 'Those mountains are built like a maze. I been lost up there myself. Unless he knew them real well he couldn't have found his way back without some kind of guide.'

'So he must have made a map.' Laura's voice brightened a little, and she turned, smiling, to face Ryker. Her breasts pressed against his arm. 'Suppose he gave each of his partners a piece. Maybe cut it into four and gave them each a bit?'

'You'd have one quarter,' said Ryker, getting interested in the idea. 'Wouldn't you?'

'No.' She shrugged, the smile leaving her face. 'Matt never gave me a piece. There was nothing like that in his papers. Only the chart he made of the whole area.'

Ryker sniffed, a new idea taking shape, building on the concept of the divided map.

'But if he sent each partner a third, then he could put them all together when it came time to open the lode. That would give him the key.'

'Yes.' She nodded thoughtfully, her eyes widening. 'That's clever of you, Jack.'

Flattered, Ryker pursued the line of the thought. 'He'd have known the general location, maybe even had it coded some way on the big map. Sending the three partners a section apiece would have been a kind of guarantee. The pieces wouldn't be any use to them, but they'd know that he was serious.'

'And they'd know that they needed to get together to find the exact spot.' Laura picked up the train of thought, expanding on it. 'Unless all the pieces were together, no one would know how to find the lode. But suppose one of them decided to take it all? Decided to get all the pieces of the map?'

'He'd have to know who the other partners were,' said Ryker. 'Studenmire and Wayne didn't sound like they knew.'

Laura gasped, fingers tightening on the gunslinger's arm.

'That could be it, Jack! That might be why Matthew was killed.'

'Why?' Ryker shrugged, not understanding. 'It don't make sense to kill the one man who knew exactly where the lode is.'

'Unless one of the partners guessed about the pieces of the map.' She took his hand, holding it tight. 'He might have guessed that Matthew had told me who the others were. If he had Matthew killed, then he could find out through me – have someone follow me. That way he'd be guided to the other two.'

It sounded plausible. Even made sense in a crazy kind of way. But mostly, Ryker wanted to believe her, because the other alternative was to believe that she was setting him up in some devious fashion. And he didn't want to think that.

'Valance,' he murmured. 'He's the only one left.'

'It has to be him.' In her excitement, Laura pressed close against his body. 'He must have planned it.'

'Yeah,' Ryker nodded. 'I guess so. Now we only got two problems.'

'What?' She looked up at him and he caught the scent she was wearing. 'Now we know the answer, we just have to get to Trinidad.'

'Without the marshal in Jefferson stopping us,' said Ryker slowly, 'and without Valance's man trying something.'

Her eyes got wide again, and her mouth opened in a smothered shriek.

'He's got to be on board,' grunted Ryker. 'And if he got Wayne's piece of the map, he doesn't need you to guide him any more.'

'Oh!' She pressed closer against him. 'I hadn't thought of that.'

'It's why you pay me,' grinned Ryker. 'All part of the service.'

Chapter Twelve

Around noon the *Missouri Princess* pulled in at Montane's Point. Two crewmen armed with Henry carbines were posted at the head of the loading ramp, and two more at the foot. The transfer of the ready-stacked timber was accomplished fast, and Abel Levant took the side-wheeler out into midstream with the boiler piling on all available power.

The riverboat kept up full speed throughout the afternoon, reaching Jefferson soon after dusk.

Levant posted guards again as he edged the boat alongside the wharf and sent a man to fetch the marshal.

Dave Farron didn't really know what to do.

The killing had happened on the river, and Farron's jurisdiction was limited to the town. There were no witnesses and too many suspects. As he pointed out to Levant, any one of the passengers might have killed Wayne. But why? There were as many crew members, and any one of them could have done it – including Levant himself.

Nathan Wayne had been known as a hard captain. The kind who sparked grudges. So maybe some disgruntled deckhand had carved him up and tossed the body over the side. Maybe – Farron suggested cautiously – Levant could have had a reason: after all he was in charge of the boat now, and the company would be looking for a new skipper. If it had been a passenger, then how the hell could Farron find out which one?

In the dead of the night. No one around. As many with solid alibis as there were with none.

Levant suggested the marshal talk with the man called Ryker and the woman he was escorting to Kansas City. They had known the captain. Joined him for dinner, and even gone back to his cabin.

By then Ryker had dropped the incriminating tool kit overboard. He hadn't enjoyed wasting good tools, but he had figured it was safest to lose what might prove to be incriminating evidence.

He told the truth when Farron questioned him.

Yes, he had spoken with Wayne. Because Mrs Tennant had a business matter to discuss with the captain. He was just a hired man.

Why? Because Mrs. Tennant's husband had been killed in Tucson and Sheriff Nolan – a personal friend of Ryker's – had suggested Mrs Tennant hire him to escort her.

A bounty hunter? Sure he was a bounty hunter. It was a reasonable living. Not that much different to being a marshal. But there wasn't any bounty on Nathan Wayne.

The business? Farron would have to ask Mrs Tennant. That was her affair, not Ryker's.

There was a certain anonymity in accepting the role of hired gun: of answering the questions with a bland smile and blank eyes. Knowing nothing except what his employer cared to tell him.

Farron talked with Laura and then gave up. He was basically a simple man, whose incumbence for the last nine years as marshal of Jefferson was based on his skill with a gun. Faced with a drunken deckhand or an angry cowboy, he knew how to handle himself. Three times he had fought off bank raids, and twice brought in wanted outlaws. But his activities and his expertise as a peace officer were contained in the clear limits of running a quiet town.

What happened on the river was boatmen's business, not his.

He told Levant that he could do nothing except report the murder to a Federal Marshal and let the suspects go.

Levant told the passengers and removed the guards. The newly-weds and two of the drummers were planning to disembark at Jefferson anyway. A third drummer and two other men chose to get off as well. They said they didn't want to travel on a jinxed boat, not one with a killer on board.

Levant suggested that Ryker and the woman wait for another passage, too. Laura informed him that she had bought tickets all the way to Kansas City and intended to see her money spent as she originally planned.

There were no new passengers.

The *Missouri Princess* churned out of the turgid waters soon after dawn. The two Army officers were still on board, along with the remaining drummer and the two women. The last of the single men stayed, too.

Ryker studied the latter carefully, remembering the description of Matthew Tennant's killer.

The man was tall and well-built. He could have been anywhere between the mid-thirties and early fifties. His hair was a uniform grey, and the pale line of an old knife-scar showed on one cheek. He wore a grey suit cut Eastern style, with button-sided boots and a wide silver-grey foulard. No gun. He ate alone and made no attempt to converse with any of the other passengers.

In fact, no one spoke much. They tended, instead, to split into solitary groups. The old woman and her companion ate their meals in nervous silence, leaving soon after to walk three times around the deck and then disappear into their shared cabin. The Army men kept their own company, while the drummer and the other man chose to remain alone.

Levant continued to wear a pistol and whenever Ryker entered the dining salon or met another passenger or crewman on the deck he was conscious of the oblique stares directed his way. It began to grate on his nerves, and only the nightly visits to Laura's cabin made the journey worthwhile.

Those and the five thousand dollars she had paid him.

Along with the desire to unravel the mystery and find the killer of the woman's husband.

They reached Kansas City at sunset.

Ryker led his horse down off the boat into a maze of wharfs and cattle pens. It was too early in the year for the southern herds to be massing, but there was already a gathering of wagons readying for the journey down the Santa Fe and Oregon trails.

He joined Laura on the sun-dried boards and slung her cases over the saddle.

'Mrs Tennant. Ryker.' He turned to see Abel Levant staring at them. 'Don't come back this way.'

'Why not?' Ryker knew the answer, but anger still prickled in his mind. 'Free passage on the river, ain't it?'

'Not on a Wayne boat.' Levant thrust his coat back, hooking his thumbs into his belt. Close to the butt of the Navy Colt. 'Not for you. I can't prove anything, but I'll pass the word along: you're no longer welcome.'

'That don't exactly break my heart,' said Ryker. 'I never liked sailors much, anyway.'

Levant shrugged, his face set in stony lines. 'Probably not, but remember what I've told you. Be best if you stayed clear of the waterfront from now on.'

It stung Ryker's pride: he wasn't used to being warned off.

'I never had much time for rats, either.'

'Jack.' The woman tugged at his sleeve. 'Please. Don't start anything.'

'No.' He took her warning. 'I won't. Not yet.'

He let her take him away into the town, helping her on to the boardwalk that flanked the wharf. It went down through a wide avenue of stockyards and warehouses into the centre of Kansas City. When they reached the outlying buildings, Ryker turned his horse into an alley and called for the woman to stop.

He waved the woman quiet, pushing her back into the shade of the overlaying porch.

A buggy had arrived to take the old woman and her daughter away. The drummer was manhandling two heavy suitcases over the boards. The Army officers were supervising a mixed gang of longshoremen and soldiers as the supplies were offloaded. And the one remaining passenger was lighting a cheroot as he watched the activity.

He had a single case with him: a black leather thing fastened by two straps.

'What's the matter?' Laura tugged at his sleeve. 'What are we waiting for?'

'I want to see where he goes,' grunted Ryker. 'I think he could be the one.'

The man tossed his match into the river and picked up the valise. Smoke curled about his face as he walked into town. As he passed the alley Ryker heard the soft sound of humming.

He waited until the man was half a block down, then stepped out into the street and followed after.

The man checked into a hotel called the *Prairie Queen*. Ryker booked into one opposite, a place with the grandiose title of the *Golden Emperor*.

It was three storeys high, and he got them rooms on the first floor, where a balcony ran out along the length of the building overlooking the street. The rooms had a connecting door and the bathroom was at the end of the corridor. The clerk gave Ryker a knowing smile as he registered their names.

The rooms were comfortable, tall windows opening on to the balcony so that the muggy air circulated under the low ceilings. There was a wide bed in each, flanked by a washstand and a wardrobe. The floors were covered with faded carpet and someone had tacked a faded daguerrotype to the wall across from Ryker's bed. It showed a woman clad in a wispy piece of lace leaning back on a brass bed with her arms open and her mouth pursed for the kiss of the camera.

Someone else had stuck tacks on her chest and scratched a hole between her legs.

Ryker tore it down and threw it on the floor.

He didn't understand why it upset him so much.

'Jack?'

He wiped his face dry and lifted the Colt from the holster slung over the bed.

Cocked the gun.

And called, 'Come in.'

Laura entered the room.

'I'm hungry,' she said, eyeing his body. 'I want to eat, and I want to know what's going on.'

Ryker grinned, dropping the pistol back in the holster.

'If that is our man,' he said, 'he'll come looking for us. The way I see it is he's got three choices. He can try something now, or on the road to Trinidad. Or try it there.'

The woman smiled, touching his chest.

'He wouldn't dare. Not with you to protect me.'

Ryker dropped the towel he was using and slid his arms around her.

'Not for a while, at least.'

She moaned deep in her throat as he picked her up and put her on the bed.

And Ryker forgot about the killings and the possible gunman and everything else; for a while.

In the morning he bought a bay mare and a saddle. Then a pack pony and sufficient provisions to carry them through to Trinidad. There had been no sign of the solitary man from the river boat, and the gunslinger was beginning to wonder if he had guessed wrong. He still thought – knew – that someone on board the *Missouri Princess* had killed Wayne for what the captain knew of the silver strike. But with no sign of any ready suspects other than the grey-haired man, he was left with only one alternative.

And as he looked down at Laura's face, eyes tight closed against the early light and hair spread in a mass of golden-brown over the pillows of the ruckled bed, he preferred not to contemplate.

He had woken her early. Watched her thrust the sheets away so that all her body was exposed, the light filtering in through the flimsy shutters outlining the curvature of her breasts and hips as she reached for him. And given up his doubts.

He had cleaned up. Shaved with the woman

watching him. And gone out to buy the horses.

Kansas City was only just waking up to breakfast as they left. There was no sign of anyone following them, nor any indication that Ryker could spot of anyone going out in front.

As a precaution, he took off on a northwards path, riding steadily for two hours before curving around to follow the line of the river westwards.

A hour later he moved south, heading down in the direction of Wichita with the intention of following the Arkansas River along to La Junta and the deep swing down to Trinidad.

Laura had left most of her luggage in Kansas City. She rode the bay pony wearing the same outfit he had seen in Houston. A dress was packed into her saddlebags, and a few more on the trailing animal. The only thing she had insisted on bringing with her was the valise.

Ryker cut back and forth across their trail, looping round and back-tracking so that the marks of their passage got mixed up and lost in a welter of indistinct hoofprints. At no time did he see anyone following them, and when he felt confident of having confused any pursuit, he set off at a fast canter to the southwest.

The one thing that preyed on his mind was the fact that whoever was trailing them would know where they were headed. And maybe be waiting there.

Like death.

But that was a thing Ryker had learned to face.

Chapter Thirteen

They skirted around Topeka and headed across country in the direction of McPherson. A few days later they picked up the loop of the Arkansas north of Hutchinson and followed the river westwards.

The Kansas plains were rich with grass, and most nights they found shelter in farms or ranch houses. Laura was an accomplished horsewoman, matching pace with Ryker so long as the willing bay was able to keep up with the big black stallion. The gunslinger travelled as swiftly as was possible, anxious to reach Trinidad and bring the mysterious affair to an end.

There was still no sign of pursuit, though that might have meant that the man on the boat had taken a more direct route. Might be waiting for them, up ahead.

If he was the one who had killed Matthew Tennant.

Ryker travelled with one hand always close to a gun and both eyes scanning the terrain. When he slept – even when Laura shared his bed – it was with a weapon under his hand and all his senses tuned to recognise danger approaching.

Spring was moving steadily closer to Summer, the rain squalls that characterised the flatlands giving way to bright, clear skies, empty of anything save the scudding clouds and the distant, dark shapes of birds.

They came to Dodge City, where Ryker sat in on

a poker game with a frail-looking man called Holliday who wore a long black overcoat even inside the saloon, and kept coughing into a stained handkerchief. Holliday's woman – an ugly girl called Kate – took a dislike to Laura, and as Holliday was close friends with the sheriff, Ryker decided to move on fast. Holliday's temper fluctuated like a summer storm and the big-nosed woman seemed to have more say with him than most other people. Ryker had no wish to cross a friend of the sheriff's so he opted to pull out earlier than planned.

West of Dodge City the country began to rise up towards the distant bulk of the Great Divide. The lush grasslands and the wheat fields gave way to sparser grass as the terrain grew rocky, and their speed slowed. It took the better part of a week before they reached La Junta and began the southern leg of their journey, down to Trinidad. They quit the river moving south in the shadow of the Sangre de Cristo range, the proximity of their destination encouraging them to forget their weariness.

And then they reached the town.

It hung between the headwaters of the Arkansas and the Canadian, sheltered by the foothills of the Rockies, with good high plains grass all around and the marks of a prosperous township sprouting two storeys high from the plateau. Wind pumps marked both ends of mainstreet, with stock pens built out around catchment tanks and stable buildings beyond. Both sides of the central street, narrower avenues ran out, flanked by houses and little gardens, or sheds and runs where pigs and chickens grubbed in the soil.

Mainstreet held a stage office, a number of stores that ranged from hardware to grain, an eating house, a saloon, an hotel, and a marshal's office.

Ryker noticed that most of the businesses carried the name of Valance.

There was Valance's Dry Goods Store; The Valance Hardware Emporium; Valance's General Store; the Valance Saddlery; Valance's Barber Shop and Bath House. The saloon was called *The Beaufort*, and the hotel was named *The Valance House*.

The town was busy, the people filling the street mostly using places with the Valance name on the front.

'Looks like he owns the town,' murmured Ryker. 'He could be hard to reach.'

'Matthew told me he has a place outside,' replied the woman. 'He doesn't come into town much.'

'What's it like?' asked Ryker. 'The house?'

'I don't know.' Laura shrugged. 'Matt never said.'

'We'll find out,' grunted Ryker. 'Maybe tomorrow.'

They booked into *The Valance House* and Ryker stabled the horses in the livery behind. That, too, belonged to Beaufort Valance.

Ryker felt a nagging dislike of the man that had nothing to do with Matthew Tennant's lost silver mine or the killings. It was just an instinctive hostility to anyone who found it necessary to spread his name around so much; to own so much. Or maybe, he reminded himself, it was just envy.

He went inside the hotel and checked his room.

It was comfortable: larger than usual with a bed and a wardrobe and a washstand, a wide window looking over the street. Laura was in the adjoining room, and as she took a bath Ryker checked his guns.

He called for hot water and soap, and while he waited he broke down the Colt and brushed it free of travel dust. Then he oiled the springs and levers and checked their tension. The pistol was built to a more complicated pattern than the Navy Colt, but its robust nature made it relatively easier to maintain. He cleaned the barrel and the cylinders, dripping a little oil inside the metal tunnels, then reassembled the handgun.

The hot water arrived and he used it to clean the two Remington Derringers, wiping both tiny pistols dry before adding a thin film of oil to the working parts.

Then he worked over the Sharps and turned to his ammunition.

There was a plentiful supply of ready-made cartridges for the heavy buffalo carbine, and an equal quantity of percussion caps. The stiff yellow paper containing the 120 grains of black powder Ryker favoured was in good condition, kept dry by his saddlebags and the waterproof lining of his pockets. He discarded a few caps that looked to be moist and began to check the .41 calibre loads of the two derringers.

Like the heavier carbine loads, the cartridges for the tiny hideaway guns were ready for use. He loaded both and tucked them back in the specially-built pouches in his right boot and belt.

There was little – except, perhaps, overlong exposure to bad weather – that could go wrong with the brass shells for the Colt's Peacemaker, but he checked each cartridge with the diligence of long-enforced habit. It was too easy to forgo such basic precautions. And too easy to die as a result.

When he was satisfied he went to take a bath, thinking about his next move as he luxuriated in the hot water.

There was only one of Matthew Tennant's partners left, which meant that only two people could be responsible for the murders dogging his trail.

From the look of Trinidad, Beaufort Valance had the money to hire an army of gunmen. And if the theory about the divided map was correct, then Valance held all the pieces. Ryker hadn't been watching for anyone on his trail until Wayne got killed on the *Missouri Princess*, but now he saw that it might have been possible.

Which pointed to Valance as the man behind the killer.

And Ryker didn't like to think about the other alternative.

Which was Laura Tennant.

She had been there when Studenmire was shot and again when Wayne died. She had known about the silver lode, and when her husband was killed she had automatically inherited all his papers.

She was tough. Her attitude when they first met and her determination to push things through to the limit proved that.

But at the same time, she had softened.

Ryker knew he was attractive to women – had enjoyed the appeal – but he had never thought of Laura as an easy bedmate. She had come to him, sure. But to a certain extent at least, it had been on her terms. And now she depended on him. Of that, he was certain. It wasn't love – at least, not on his part – but on both sides he felt it was something more than just lustful usage.

And if Laura was using him, how could she hope to handle the current situation?

She knew he wasn't a simple hired gun, ready to pistol down any target she pointed out. So if she had tricked him all the way down the line to the last partner, what was she planning now? What could she plan? Valance looked to have the town sewn up, and she couldn't hope to kill the man and blame it on Ryker. Nor to ride free without more questions than were comfortable being asked.

No.

Ryker laughed at himself: it couldn't be that way. He was just getting nervy; suspicious of everyone. Laura had broken him out of jail in Houston and been ready to give him an alibi on the river.

It couldn't be her. So it had to be Beaufort Valance.

The gunslinger climbed out of the tub and began to dry his body. He whistled softly as a plan formed in his mind.

The eating house was one of the few places that didn't belong to Valance. And it served good food.

Ryker chewed steak as he outlined his plan.

Laura listened, cutting her meal into dainty mouthfuls as her eyes got wide and concerned.

'But if we just ride in there anything could happen. Jack, he *must* be the one, so he'll be expecting us. He'll have us killed.'

'Not if he knows we told the marshal first,' said Ryker. 'If we go see the lawman in the morning and explain what's happened – leastways about your husband getting killed and how the others died – he's got to start worrying about Valance.'

'He'll arrest us.'

'No.' Ryker shook his head. 'No way he can. We're in Colorado now. Texas killings are way out of his jurisdiction. Same applies for the river. All we do is buy some free insurance.'

'I think it might be best if we left the law out of this,' she murmured, changing her mind. 'So far it's only got us into difficulties. Why can't we just ride out to his house and face him?'

'Because,' said Ryker; patiently, 'he looks to own this town. That means he can buy the law and run a private army.'

'So telling the marshal is just like giving ourselves away.' The woman sipped coffee, her eyes clouding with concern. 'He'll stop us.'

'No.' Ryker shook his head. 'We'll write a letter tonight. Say what's happened and how we're going out to Valance's place come morning. We leave copies in the bank and the mailbox down at the stage office. And we tell the marshal what we done. That way he has to protect us, even if Valance is paying him off.'

'I don't agree.' She set down her cup, her eyes beginning to get angry. 'Valance can buy off either letter. Or steal them.'

'Be too risky.' Ryker smiled, enjoying his coffee and his idea. 'He might influence the bank, but he'll have problems with the US Mail.'

Laura frowned: 'I think you're wrong. I think we should go straight in to his place without telling anyone.'

'That's crazy.' Ryker felt the first stirrings of anger. 'That way we could both get killed and no questions asked.'

'I don't like it,' said Laura. 'Not at all.'

Ryker shrugged: 'You paid me five thousand to see this through. You want to call it off?'

'No!' She shook her head vigorously. 'I don't want to stop it now. It's gone too far. And I need you to finish it.'

'Then we do it my way.' Ryker drained his cup. 'Or not at all.'

Marshal Dell Brown was the kind of man who liked insurance.

He knew his tenure in office came from the townsfolk of Trinidad as much as it did from the wallets of the rich people. Beaufort Valance, Jimmy Lawrence and Telford Harkness might be the biggest ranchers around, but there were still the small folk. The ones who voted when the elections came up. And Dell Brown wasn't about to offend them.

He read through Ryker's letter with his lips moving carefully over every word. Then looked up at Laura's breasts and Ryker's eyes.

'An' you left one o' these at the bank an' one in the mailbox at the stage office?'

Ryker nodded.

'Ain't nuthin' but a deposition so far,' said Brown. 'Mister Valance could use that against you if he was the one got killed, an' I ain't about to police your lives.'

'But you will assure us you'll guard against attacks?' said Laura. 'You'll see we get there safely?'

'With my own eagle eye, ma'am.' Brown tapped the star on his chest. 'I look after folk.'

He stood up from behind his desk.

'Tell you what. I'll ride out there now. See you safely on to Valance land. Then if you don't come back. I'll go up an' ask some questions.'

'Thanks,' said Ryker. 'Thanks a lot.'

The Valance house was built out from a spur of the Sangre de Cristo range like an eagle's nest.

West of Trinidad, the trail wound up through rich grasslands to a fork of the mountains. One spur bled off in a long southwards curve, while the other jutted out to the east like a bird's talon. The house was built out over the vertical face of the hill, just above a tumbling watercourse.

There was a narrow trail leading in – a wooden bridge spanning the stream – and a fenced plateau. Palomino ponies grazed on the flat, their colours matching the weathered facing of the house.

The building itself was supported on stone piles so that one section jutted out over the downslopes just above the water. There was a balcony set there, enormous windows looking down towards the town. On the south side a staircase led down to the ground, the well descending on to a stone-covered patio where a massive door gave access to the interior.

Two men with Remington shotguns came out from the shadows as Brown led the way in.

The marshal waved a greeting, and one man called something over his shoulder, into the house.

'You're on yore own now,' said Brown. 'I done all I can. Ain't no way I can ensure your safety any more.'

He turned his horse around and rode fast over the bridge, scattering a trio of grazing palominos as he thundered clear of the impressive house.

Ryker climbed down and helped Laura from the saddle.

'I'm frightened,' she whispered. 'You'll look after me, won't you?'

'Sure.' He watched the men with the scatterguns, wondering how much protection a pistol might afford against that kind of fire-power. 'Sure I'll look after you.'

A head poked out from behind the door and one of the guards waved them forwards.

'The boss'll see you now.'

Ryker passed the reins of their horses to the second man and stepped inside the house.

There was a vast hall, the floor covered with Spanish tiles, the walls with wooden panels. Doors opened off the enormous room and a wide staircase led up one side. At the far end there was a huge open fireplace.

The servant who had spoken to the guard ushered them both to the massive table at the centre of the floor and filled two glasses from the decanter in the middle.

Ryker sipped the drink and grimaced.

'What the hell is it?'

'Sherry, Jack.' Laura drank hers with relish. 'A fine drink.'

'The finest! But I'd not expect a hired gunman to understand the niceties of such delicate matters.'

Ryker spun round, lifting up from his seat with the Colt cocked and ready in his hand.

'Please.' The voice was deep, echoing off the walls. 'Put the gun away. I'd hate to spoil my floor with blood.'

There was no way of telling where the sound came from. It rang all round the room, bouncing off the walls and rattling on the glasses. Ryker turned slowly, ready to fire. Watching the doors and the staircase.

Laura sat with her glass clenched tight in white-knuckled fingers. She was chewing her lower lip, and tiny beads of sweat were bursting from her forehead.

'There's nothing you can do,' bellowed the voice. 'So sit down. If it makes you feel safer, keep your gun in your hand. But don't try to use it. If you do, you're dead.'

Ryker sat down, dropping the Colt back in the holster.

He put both hands on the table and said, 'All right. What now?'

'Now we talk,' said the voice. 'About why you're

here with Matthew Tennant's widow. And what I shall do with you. Both of you.'

There was the sound of footsteps on stone, then the warmer sound of leather on wood. Ryker turned towards the staircase.

And fought to keep his face still as he stared at the grotesque parody of a man that hobbled down the stairs.

'I am Beaufort Valance.' He was obviously accustomed to the effect he produced, for something vaguely like a smile puckered his lips. 'You're a brave man to come here. Or a fool. I wonder which?'

Ryker decided it was the latter as Valance turned to Laura and said, 'Won't you introduce us, my dear? I've been looking forward to this meeting.'

Chapter Fourteen

Beaufort Valance walked with the aid of two heavy sticks. His right foot was encased in an oversized shoe, the sole three inches thick to compensate for the uneven length of his legs. His shoulders were bulked out with muscle, jutting either side of a scrawny neck that supported a head that looked like a stampeding herd had run over the face. One eye was half-closed, the lid obviously sewn in place so that it overhung the pupil, dragging the eye down at an angle. His nose had been broken in several places and set crooked, the tip twisted round to point at the horseshoe scar on his cheek. His jaw, too, looked to have been broken, for it was out of line with the rest of his face, the mouth twisted so that several yellowish teeth protruded over the upper lip. His skull was a patchwork of pink scar tissue and wispy white hair that grew in little tufts, like fungus.

He turned his good eye on Ryker, twisting his obscene head to bring the gunslinger into focus. And chuckled.

Ryker stared at the woman, his own face twisting into ugly lines as the sudden rage that had given him his nickname of Black Jack Ryker began to possess him.

Laura smiled nervously; incongruously.

'Beaufort Valance; Jack Ryker.'

'Only my friends call me Jack,' he grated. 'You

goddam lying bitch!'

Laura blushed, avoiding his angry gaze.

'In case you're thinking of giving way to a perfectly natural desire to kill her,' said Valance, 'let me point out the men I have posted here.'

He balanced on one stick, lifting the other to indicate the walls. Sections of the pine cladding had swung open to expose a series of small windows overlooking the room. A man hung over each sill, Winchester rifles cocked and pointing on the gunslinger.

Ryker clenched his fists, then lowered them slowly back to the table.

'Why?' he asked. 'Why go through all this?'

Valance lowered himself into a heavy chair of carved oak and rested his sticks against the table. As he filled a glass, Ryker saw that three fingers were missing from his left hand. He sipped the sherry, nodding his approval. And began to speak.

'I wasn't born like this, Ryker. And I don't enjoy looking like this now. I was once a handsome man. Tall, like you. One for the ladies. Laura here was one of them.' He ducked his head in the woman's direction, chuckling again as she averted her eyes. 'You see? She remembers. Remembers the days back in Washington when I courted her. Oh, I danced then, and I could talk. I had my pick of the girls, but the only one I wanted was Laura. Laura Harvey – the belle of Washington society.'

He paused, emptying his glass and filling it again.

'There were two of us felt that Miss Harvey might accept our suit: Matthew and I. We were friends. Close friends. We sent her flowers. We wined her and dined and danced with her. We were the talk of Washington social circles: the lovely Miss Laura Harvey and her two beaux. Everyone wondered who she would choose.

'Then the war came. Matthew and I enlisted immediately. It was the thing to do. And besides, Laura urged us to. She told us she couldn't decide between us; that she would marry the one who proved himself in the fighting. It was all very romantic, and we thought the war couldn't last longer than a few months. We were assigned to the Engineers.'

He drained his glass and poured a fresh measure. Ryker noticed that his eyes were blue. And very cold.

'It was in Pennsylvania. The Confederates were pushing north and we were detailed to slow their progress. There was a godforsaken little town called Andaheim. Just a few houses and a bridge. The bridge was very important, because it was the only easy crossing of the river. We set our charges and sent the men back. Matt and I stayed to light the fuses.

'I was handling the charges under the bridge. The ones fastened to the stanchions. Matt was handling the topside. We'd agreed that he should give me a ten-minute start – enough time to prime and light. He gave me three minutes before he set match to fuse.'

His hands clenched, slopping sherry over the polished wood of the table.

'The whole damn' thing blew up on me. I still can remember the roar of it. The flames. Remember falling into that dirty water. I woke up in a military hospital with bandages all over me and pain all through me.

'I was there for six months. Then they sent me back to Washington and kept me in a hospital for another year. When they let me out, I looked like this.'

He leaned back in his chair, distorted shoulders

pushing his neck forwards so that he resembled a vulture.

'I knew that Miss Laura Harvey wouldn't look at me, and I found that my family didn't like to have me around. They offered me money to go away. "Why not tour Europe?" they said. "There are very good doctors over there." I refused. I took the money they offered and came out here. I built this house and began to buy into the town. I am a very good businessman, Ryker. Very good, indeed.

'And business can keep a man in touch with events. I heard that Laura had married Matthew, and I decided that it was time he paid for crippling me. I speculated on the stock market, parlayed my money up until I was in a position to buy into certain organisations that influence the Army and its civilian associates. I controlled Matthew Tennant's company. I owned him! There wasn't a dime he wasted on gambling or women that I didn't know about. And he spent plenty on both. But never without me getting the final accounting!'

'Did you know this?' Ryker turned to the woman. 'Were you lying to me all along?'

She shook her head, eyes filling with tears. 'No. Matthew never told me about his business arrangements. It wasn't until we got to Tucson I even knew Beau was still alive.'

Valance chuckled some more. 'She's telling the truth, Ryker. Up to a point, at least. She really did think I was dead. "Killed in action", Matt told her. "Died fighting the rebels." It wasn't until he told me about the silver that I revealed myself.'

'Why?' Ryker asked for the second time, feeling like a child in school who can't see the answer to a problem everyone else finds obvious. 'I don't understand.'

'Because I wanted to destroy Matthew Tennant,' snarled Valance, 'I could have destroyed him financially any time I chose, but that wouldn't have been enough. I wanted him to lose every way possible. I wanted him to suffer the way I've suffered since he tried to kill me on that goddam bridge.

'Finding that silver was the key to his own destruction. He was greedy, you see. He spent most of what he made on women or gambling. Laura didn't know about that. Not until I told her. And that gave her a shock. You see, she'd always thought her husband was the dutiful type. Thought he loved her and his trips west were just unpleasant duties. She didn't know about the money he lost on Wayne's riverboats or the women he had every place he stayed.

'He had the one woman I wanted, Ryker. But she wasn't enough. He couldn't even satisfy himself with whores. No, he needed mistresses. Women waiting to see him again. There was one in St Louis. Another in Chicago. One in Phoenix and another in San Antonio. I had him watched – the Pinkertons are very good – and when the time was right I showed the evidence to Laura. At least, I sent a man to show it to her.

'That was when she agreed to help me. In return for half the silver strike, of course. That's one fault the belle of Washington has: she is greedy.'

'He fooled me,' murmured Laura. 'He lied to me and tricked me all those years. He had it coming.'

'I got word he was in Tucson,' continued Valance, 'so I knew he was getting ready to move. He'd already sent me a piece of the map and told me there were two other partners. He thought that he could fool me. Buy me out. He thought that if I didn't have all the map, I'd not be able to move against him. He didn't know his own wife was on my side.'

'Jesus!' Ryker's mouth gaped open in surprise. 'You mean you set the whole thing up? All the way?'

'It was an obvious plan,' shrugged Valance, lifting his warped shoulders higher than his head. 'But it went slightly wrong. I had intended to frighten Matt into running to the other partners, but the man I sent overstepped his duties: he killed the bastard! Neither Laura nor I knew the exact location of the strike, so it was necessary to find the others and take their pieces of the map. At the same time, we both needed to stay clear of possible recriminations. That was why Laura hired you.'

Ryker's mouth snapped shut. Settled into a tight line. He leaned back, resting his fingers on the edge of the table as he scanned the rifles pointing from the openings in the walls.

'It was her idea,' said Valance. 'And quite brilliant. She suggested that we find some local gunman willing to escort her to each of the partners. A man known to kill for money. Your name came up.'

'Who killed them?' Ryker asked coldly. 'Who killed Studenmire and Wayne?'

'Laura, of course,' said Valance. 'She really is a most remarkable woman.'

'Yeah.' Ryker looked at the woman again. 'Remarkable.'

There was the bitter taste of defeat in his mouth. Like sour ashes mingled with blood. He felt angry and confused. Most of all, he felt ashamed: he had been used. Used like a puppet with the woman pulling his strings. He didn't like that.

He scratched his right leg.

'You shouldn't blame yourself too much, Ryker,' said Valance. 'After all, Laura is a very persuasive woman. And you did get five thousand dollars from the deal.'

'You gonna let me spend it?' Ryker asked. 'Or do I know too much?'

'I've been wondering about that,' said Valance. 'What do you think, Laura?'

'He's too honest.' Her voice sounded flat, almost regretful. 'If it was anyone else, I'd buy them off.'

'Five thousand should buy off most men,' said Valance.

'Not Jack Ryker.' Laura raised her head, looking into his eyes. 'I'm sorry, Jack, but it can't be any other way.'

Ryker scratched his leg some more, working down from the kneecap to the top of his boot.

'So you'll have me killed,' he grunted. 'Just like that.'

'We don't have any choice,' said the woman. 'You'd not walk away knowing you've been used. I know you too well to believe that.'

'Yeah. I guess you should know me pretty well by now.' Ryker lifted the little Remington from his boot holster and folded his hands. It looked like he was giving up and clenching his fists in frustration. The movement hid the tiny pistol as he rested both fists on his thighs.

'He left a letter,' said Laura. 'It tells what happened.'

'He should have added a bit,' said Valance. 'About how he tried to kill me and my foreman shot him down. Yates!'

A tall man with grey hinting the sides of his temples came into the room. He wore a black suit, the tails hiked back to expose a cutaway holster. The sharply curved butt and outstanding trigger spur of a Smith & Wesson Russian protruded from the leather. A fine, whitish knife-scar ran down one side of his face.

'Mister Valance?' His voice was deep and calm. 'What shall I do with him?'

'Take him out and kill him,' said Valance. 'Then bring me that pistol he carries.'

'Might be an idea to do it here,' suggested Yates. 'It'd look better.'

Laura nodded. 'He's right. Don't forget that Ryker left a letter.'

'All right.' Valance nodded. 'In here then.'

He glanced round the windows in the walls and shouted, 'Get out! Shut those windows.'

The pine planks thudded back in place and the hall fell silent. Yates drew the Smith & Wesson, curling his forefinger around the trigger, the second digit cupping the underslung trigger spur.

Ryker tensed as the hammer went back, the triple *click* sounding loud in the quiet room.

'Put your gun on the table, Ryker. Use your left hand.'

Ryker eased his left arm across his belly and drew the Colt out.

'Slow an' easy. Don't try anything.'

He set it on the polished wood.

'Push it away.'

He pushed, watching the gun skid over the surface to clatter against the decanter.

'That's good. Now, let's get it done.'

Yates turned the Smith & Wesson and fired once. Ryker went back in his chair, tilting the heavy thing far enough over that he was able to power sideways across the arm. He expected to feel a bullet hit him, calculating the angle and speed of his drop and coming up with the probability of a shoulder wound on the right side.

So he dropped the Remington derringer into his left hand.

He hit the floor as the Russian thundered once.

Heard someone scream.

Felt a chair pitch over.

For an instant Beaufort Valance's good eye stared at him. Then the hole in the centre of the cripple's forehead gouted blood that dripped down to cover the orb. The man was lying sideways in the chair, his twisted mouth gaping wide in surprise and pain. Spittle dribbled from his jaw, the yellow mucous staining red as blood pulsed from the hole in his ghastly face.

Ryker fired without thinking, pointing the derringer at the legs of the black-clad man.

Yates and Laura screamed together.

The gunman fell down with the splinters of his shattered ankle sticking out from his left boot. He cocked the Russian and triggered a wild shot as Ryker powered clear, moving for the stairs.

Laura picked up the Colt, holding the pistol in both hands as she thumbed the hammer back and swung the muzzle in Ryker's direction.

The gunslinger reached the stairs and found cover behind the balustrade.

Yates triggered two shots that splintered wood without going through. Laura fired once, the Colt bucking in her hands to plough splinters from the wall behind Ryker's position.

'You bastard!' she screamed. 'You goddam fucking bastard! You spoiled it all.'

'What?' Ryker shouted. 'Tell me.'

Yates moaned and began to drag himself under the big table. His broken ankle left a long trail of blood that mingled with the crimson still pulsing from Valance's face.

'You're dead, Jack!' Her voice carried the hysterical edge of total panic. 'You know that. I set you up all along. Then you had to spoil it. You should have killed Beaufort. That would have made it simple.'

'For who?' shouted Ryker. 'You or me?'

'For us both,' she screamed. 'You were meant to shoot Beau.'

'An' then get shot myself?' called Ryker. 'That don't sound like a good deal.'

'You could've shot Yates,' wailed the woman. 'I was only using him to get back at Beau. If only you'd killed him too, we might've had all that silver for ourselves. Kill him now, Jack. We'll go off together. You know I'm good for you.'

'You goddam fucking bitch!' Yates turned the Smith & Wesson in Laura's direction. 'You lyin' fucking cow!'

He squeezed the trigger.

Laura screamed as the .44 calibre slug bit upwards through her ribcage. It went in low down on her back, plucking between the fly ribs to emerge from between her breasts in a sticky spray of crimson that gouted over the table, colouring the sherry glasses with the rich tint of life.

Yates fired again, his second shot driving through the woman's pelvic girdle and out through her stomach. It jerked her body forwards over the table, arms outstretched and fingers opening so that the Colt was pushed forwards over the far edge to slither across the floor.

She moaned, her hips jerking in an obscene parody of sex as blood pumped from her chest and belly. The decanter and glasses toppled to the floor, glass shattering as sticky trailers of blood ran down from the woodwork to stain the tiles and briefly glinting shards.

Ryker fired the derringer once and dropped the pistol inside his pocket as he rolled down the stairs.

He grabbed the Colt and thumbed the hammer back, holding the gun close to the floor as he sighted on Yates.

The gunman was stretched out under the table with the Smith & Wesson poking over the underpinning. He squeezed the trigger as Ryker's face showed around the foot of the stairs.

The bullet splintered wood three inches over Ryker's head.

And Yates thumbed the locking catch that sprung the hinged cylinder clear of the butt plate. The spent shells jumped into the air, emptying faster than was possible with a Colt.

Yates reached down to his belt and began to feed fresh shells into the chambers.

Ryker cocked the Colt and fired once.

His bullet hit Yates on the topside of the forehead. It scored a bloody line down the man's face, glancing off the curve of bone to rip through his nostrils and blast into the open cylinder of the Smith & Wesson. The impact detonated the loaded cartridges. And the gun blew up.

It exploded on each cylinder Yates had loaded. And he loaded fast.

Five chambers blasted powder and overheated metal back into the man's face. It was like five bullets hitting him at the same time. His scream got lost in the explosion and his face got hidden in the reeking cloud of smoke.

When it cleared he was slumped on the floor. His eyes were black pits that oozed blood and smoke. His nose was gone, and his lips were shredded back from his blackened teeth. Blood and smoke and sticky pieces of metal dribbled from his mangled jaw. His hair smouldered.

Ryker stood up and went over to the table.

Yates mumbled something, and the gunslinger bent down trying to catch his words.

He wasn't sure he heard it right, but it sounded like, 'Tell Laura I love her.'

'Tell her yourself.' Ryker glanced at the woman's body. 'In hell.'

'Oh, sweet Jesus!' Frothy pink blood bubbled from Yates's mouth, getting darker as he coughed. He lifted both hands to his ruined face, and moaned as powder-blackened nails touched the exposed bone on his cheeks and jaw. 'I wish I'd never listened to her.'

'Me too.' Ryker's voice was bitter. 'But she had a sweet tongue.'

He began to reload the Colt as Yates's head fell back. Twin streamers of blood spurted from the pits where the man's nostrils had been, and a thicker flow erupted from his mouth. His heels drummed briefly on the floor, their movement disturbing the flies that were clustering on Valance's face and Laura's back. Then he was still.

A door opened and a man came into the room. He was dressed like a cowhand and he looked like he knew how to use the Winchester he was pointing at Ryker's belly.

'You'd best send for the marshal,' grunted Ryker.. 'Now.'

The man nodded, eyes gaping wide as he stared at the three bodies. 'You wait right here.'

Ryker shrugged as two more cowboys came into the room. He located a cabinet that looked like it would hold liquor and opened it. No one stopped him, so he poured a big measure of whisky and downed the alcohol in one fast swallow. Then he refilled the glass and sat down at the end of the table. The blood was drying on Valance's face and the flies had turned their attentions to the spray of brain matter behind the shattered skull. Yates's corpse was still oozing crimson, but the stains covering the back of Laura's riding habit were drying to a uniform brown. It matched the original colour.

Her face was turned in Ryker's direction, the hazel eyes wide open and the full lips parted. She still looked beautiful. Except for the drying streamer of blood plastering her lower lip.

The gunslinger swallowed more whisky and turned away from the sightless stare.

Trinidad was dark by the time Ryker and Brown got back.

They went up to Laura's room and opened the valise she had hidden in the wardrobe. It contained close on fifteen thousand dollars and a close-detail map of the Superstition range. There were also two pieces of a hand-drawn map with reference points inked in and instructions inscribed neatly down the margin.

'That'd be worth havin',' murmured Brown. 'If what you told me is right.'

'You'd need Valance's section,' said Ryker, slowly. 'And he never did say where that was.'

'So it's one more dream got lost.' Brown shrugged, striking a match to light his pipe. 'How many got killed fer those bits of paper?'

'Tennant and the man he was with,' Ryker murmured. 'An old man in Tucson. Colby Studenmire and his boyfriend. Nathan Wayne. Valance and Yates. And the woman.'

'Christ!' Brown took the pipe from his mouth. 'That's nine.'

'Yeah.' Ryker tore the paper across three times and took the match from Brown's fingers. 'There was a couple more back in Houston.' He set flame to the edge. 'That makes it eleven.'

The paper burned crisply. The flames took hold and browned the lower part. Ryker dropped the pieces into the empty washbasin and watched as they blackened and began to curl. Soon there was nothing left except ashes. He stirred them with his finger.

'Now there ain't anyone gonna find it.' said Brown. 'Not ever.'

'Not until the next time,' grated Ryker. 'And there's usually a next time.'

In the morning he sold the pack horse and the woman's bay mare. They fetched two hundred dollars with the equipment they carried.

It was a bright morning, the sky clear and blue. He rode southwards wondering how Sheriff Nolan could persuade the authorities in Houston to drop the charges against him.

He hoped Nolan could find a way.

BETTER TIMES THAN THESE

BY WINSTON GROOM

The shattering classic novel of a dirty war

'Bravo' company, U.S. Seventh Cavalry. Raw recruits and ambitious commanders. Men with the tradition of General Custer and the Indian wars behind them. This is the story of another bloody chapter in American history: the battle of Ia Drang valley, and of the soldiers who fought there. But it is more than the story of those soldiers: it tells of the world – and the women – they left behind them, and of what happened when they came up against the horrors of combat. It shocks, horrifies, moves and enthralls – because it always tells the raw truth.

'A mirror of hell that leaves one awestruck'
NEW YORK TIMES

'A thoroughly realistic portrait of men at war . . . frightening . . . genuinely merits comparison with James Jones'
PUBLISHERS WEEKLY

WAR 0 7221 4100 9 £1.75

ARENA

BY NORMAN BOGNER

IN THE NEW WORLD THEY STARTED NEW LIVES, WITH NEW NAMES – AND A DREAM THAT WAS AS OLD AS MANKIND . . .

In the beginning there were the four families, driven together by a common enemy, united by the dream they shared. Together they fled to their 'promised land'. There, with new names and new hopes, they went their own ways but always connected by a chain of love and danger. And each would play a part in the intrigues, the dealing and dying, the loving and losing that meant –

ARENA

Sweeping from a daring bank raid in the heart of Hitler's Germany to a breathtaking bid for power at the topmost level of America's greatest sporting enterprise, from the pain and sweat of the fight business to the splendour and decadence of the movie industry, from the inevitable, brutal consummation of a merciless underworld vendetta to the tender consummation of a love that miraculously survived the most turbulent events of the Twentieth Century, ARENA is a genuine blockbuster of a novel from one of the greatest storytellers of our time.

GENERAL FICTION 0 7221 1733 7 £1.75

SNOW FALCON

BY CRAIG THOMAS

WHILE RUSSIA AND AMERICA TALK PEACE, THE WORLD'S MIGHTIEST WAR MACHINE IS READYING ITSELF FOR THE ULTIMATE ACT OF WAR . . .

In London, British Intelligence possess the tortured ramblings of a dying Russian tank commander . . . and in Moscow the KGB anxiously listen to a mysterious taped phone call made by a dead civil servant.

Both refer to 'Group 1917'

In a few days the Helsinki Summit will take place at which the Salt 3/Mars Treaty will be ratified between America and Russia. The Red Army are openly violently opposed to the agreement.
Gambling on a hunch that tenuously links the random events, British Intelligence dispatches agents – codenamed *Snow Falcon* – to the Finnish border and desperately awaits information. For if *Snow Falcon* fails to report the balance of world power faces TOTAL DEADLY DESTRUCTION.

SNOW FALCON, Craig Thomas's latest blockbusting thriller, is the stunningly well researched story of political conspiracy and international espionage set in the frozen climes of the North. Tense and superbly compelling it propels the reader to a nerve-shattering climax, a hair's-breadth away from tomorrow's world.

And don't miss Craig Thomas's other bestselling thrillers
FIREFOX
RAT TRAP
WOLFSBANE
Also available from Sphere Books

GENERAL FICTION 0 7221 854 9 £1.50

BY GRAHAM MASTERTON

RICH IS POWER!

RICH IS PASSION!

RICH IS PRIVILEGE!

RICH IS EXPLOSIVE!

RICH is the story of a family that grew from poverty and innocence . . . to become wealthy, beautiful – and damned.

Follow their incredible ascent through seven sprawling decades, in a thrilling saga that springs to life from the pen of Graham Masterton, the most exciting new story-teller since Harold Robbins!

Get RICH quick . . . read Graham Masterton's blockbusting new novel RICH

FICTION 0 7221 5988 9 £1.95